Mates, Dates & Saving The Planet

Cathy Hopkins lives in London with her husband and two cats, Emmylou and Otis. The cats appear to be slightly insane. Their favourite game is to run from one side of the house to the other as fast as possible, then see if they can fly if they leap high enough off the furniture. This usually happens at three o'clock in the morning and they usually land on anyone who happens to be asleep at the time. Cathy has had a chat with them about going green and they have agreed to do what they can to bring down their carbon pawprint.

Cathy spends most of her time locked in a shed at the bottom of the garden pretending to write books but is actually in there listening to music, hippie dancing and checking her Facebook page.

Apart from that, Cathy has joined the gym and spends more time than is good for her making up excuses as to why she hasn't got time to go.

Cathy Hopkins

Mates, Dates & Saving The Planet

A girl's guide to being green and gorgeous!

Thanks to ... *he fab team at Pi...* ... *er for her researc* ... *Sue Hellard for* ... *th for her expert* ...

First published in Great Britain in 2008
by Piccadilly Press Ltd, 5 Castle Road,
London NW1 8PR

Text copyright © Cathy Hopkins and Vic Parker 2008
Illustrations copyright © Sue Hellard 2008

A catalogue record for this book is available from the British Library

ISBN: 978 1 85340 966 0 (trade paperback)

1 3 5 7 9 10 8 6 4 2

Printed and bound by CPI Bookmarque, Croydon
Designed by Fiona Webb
Cover design by Simon Davis

Papers used by Piccadilly Press are produced from forests grown
and managed as a renewable resource, and which conform to the
requirements of recognised forestry accreditation schemes.

Mixed Sources
Product group from well-managed
forests and other controlled sources
FSC   www.fsc.org   Cert no. TT-COC-002227
© 1996 Forest Stewardship Council

Contents

Department for Education

DISCLAIMER NOTICE

The DfE accepts no responsibility for the incomplete or incorrect information contained in this non-fiction publication. All citizens are free to accept or not the information contained herein. The Department's duty to provide accurate information in the education of its citizens and, especially, its children is discharged with this notice which makes clear that eating animal protein (ie meat, fish, eggs and dairy) significantly increases the risk of cancer, heart disease, diabetes and early death. Vegan diets, rich in high-fibre plant foods, create the lowest risk for these diseases.

It should also be noted that animal agriculture produces more greenhouse gases than all transport put together; it is also by far the biggest cause of rainforest destruction and ocean deadzones.

Introduction

A Note from Lucy

'So what are we going to do to save the planet then?' asked Izzie one Saturday afternoon recently when we (Izzie, TJ, Nesta and me, Lucy) were sitting in Costa's in Highgate.

'What?' said Nesta as she licked chocolate off her spoon then took a sip of her cappuccino.

'We need to do something about global warming,' said Izzie.

'Nah,' said Nesta. 'Bring it on, I say. It means we get fab weather. No more freezing winters. More chances to wear my bikini, look cool in my shades and get a tan. I'm all for it.'

'But what about the polar bears?' asked TJ.

'What *about* the polar bears?' asked Nesta.

'They will probably be extinct within one hundred years if it carries on.'

'So? We'll be extinct too,' said Nesta. 'Like do you really care what happens in a hundred years? We won't be around.'

'Yes, but our children and grandchildren will be,' said Izzie.

'So let them sort it out,' said Nesta.

'I'm not having children,' I said. 'Way too messy. But I do think we should think about it at least, like, how can we stop global warming?'

'We can't. We're fifteen-year-old schoolgirls,' said Nesta.

'Ah, but remember that quote,' said Izzie. *'If you think you're too small to have any effect, just think what one mosquito can do.'*

'Oh come on, don't let's get heavy,' said Nesta as she clocked a cute boy who'd just walked in. 'It's the weekend. Let's just stick with what we're good at. Being teenagers, checking out boys and then doing a spot of window shopping.'

'That's what *you're* good at,' said Izzie. 'Some of us want to make a difference.'

'Oo-er, get her,' said Nesta.

'I agree with Izzie,' said TJ. 'I think we should do our bit and there must be something we can do. Anything's better than nothing.'

'Bor-ing,' groaned Nesta.

And then Izzie played her master card. 'I was listening to Luke and William talking about it the other night. They're going to see what they can do. William is really into it. I've noticed that a lot of boys seem to take this whole green thing seriously.'

Hah! That got Nesta's attention. William and Luke are major cute boys and William just happens to be Nesta's boyfriend (and Luke is TJ's). Plus

Nesta's always had this complex that she might be a bit shallow and as William is really clever, she worries sometimes that he may dump her.

'OK, *OK*. So what can we do then?' she asked.

And that's what got us started.

I have to admit we used to be total ignoramuses when it came to the environment and all things green. But then we began to notice that we couldn't turn on the TV or radio or open a magazine without some scientist telling us urgently that climate change is real, it is here, and it's threatening life as we know it. Pretty gloomy doomy news. But there's some good news too and that is scientists also believe that it's not too late for action – so long as we act *now*.

After that afternoon, we all decided to go off and think up as many ways as possible to help and TJ suggested doing this guide to being green. And so, we're proud to present you with the results right here. You may be worrying that saving the planet means you'll have to start drinking your bath water, let your legs grow hairy and stop using lip gloss. Well, you can if you really want to, but you don't have to. Oh no – we found out that there are all sorts of things you can do that will make a difference to the environment without causing yourself any hardship. Going green doesn't mean that you can never travel in a car again. Or that you should sit at home with all the lights and the heating off – and preferably the TV off too . . . You just need a bit of thought and effort from time to time. One person really *can* make a difference. We (even Nesta) will show you how.

Lots of love
Lucy

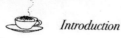

PS A note from Nesta while the others aren't listening: *I am sure a lot of you out there are like me. Like, I said I'd go green but I don't want anyone droning on, boring me with the facts. I get it. Planet is in trouble. We're using up our natural resources. We have to act. My attitude is: just tell me what to do. And don't go on about it. Puleese.*

We won't – Izzie, TJ, Lucy.

Oh, you heard. OK. Lalallalala – Nesta.

PPS There's a Glossary at the back of this book which explains eco words you may come across and may not be sure of. We're helpful like that, you know . . .

CHAPTER 1

How Green Are You?

A Note from Izzie

Hi. It's Izzie here.

First of all, a humungous thank you for picking up this book. You are a very good person for this and will get mucho mucho good karma. (For those of you who don't know, karma is not a chicken curry, that's korma; no, karma is like collecting reward points at Sainsbury's – kind of – you get back what you put in sort of thing.) Anyway, you are a good person. All the animals in the world thank you. All the plants in the world thank you. All the living things in the oceans thank you. All the future generations of the human race thank you. They will build statues to you and worship you. OK, maybe not.

Second of all, we may be just a small band of mates, but together we can rock the world. I mean, look at that popstar Bob Geldof; he phoned up a few of his pals and organised the Live 8 concerts in 2005 – five days afterwards, the leaders of eight of the world's richest countries pledged to double 2004 levels of aid to the poorest nations on Earth. Don't get me wrong, I'm not saying I think that we can solve the world's problems by tomorrow teatime. But we can definitely help – and have some great times together while we're doing it.

To start with, I've put together a personality quiz about how you live your life and the choices you make every day (maybe without even realising it) about the environment. Answer the questions and keep a tally of your rating (a, b or c for each question), then check the scores ratings at the end. You'll find out whether you're an eco-wombat, an eco-worrier or an eco-superhero.

Love and peace,

Izzie XX

Are you an eco-superhero?

♡ 1. How much do you recycle?
   a. Recycle what?
   b. Not much – I'm not sure what to do.
   c. Almost everything! I am known as Ramona the Recycling Queen.

♡ 2. What's your most regular mode of transport?
   a. Car.
   b. The bus/train/tube/tram.
   c. Walking or cycling.

♡ 3. When you go to the supermarket do you . . .
   a. Use the plastic carrier bags they provide – that's what they're there for.
   b. Bring back your plastic bags from the previous shop because you get money back for using them again.
♡ c. Bring your own big bag or a cardboard box with you every time.

♡ 4. How many protest letters have you ever written about green issues?
   a. None. Are you joking?
   b. I did think about it, but I never got round to it.
   c. One or more.

♡ 5. What did you do with your last old mobile phone?
  a. Binned it.
  b. Traded it in at the shop as part of the deal for
     my new one.
  c. Gave it to a phone recycling scheme.

♡ 6. What's your attitude to organic food?
  a. It's expensive.
  b. I eat organic stuff whenever I can.
  c. I grow my own organic veggies – you can
     really taste the difference.

♡ 7. You've finished doing your homework on your
  computer and you can hear the theme tune to your
  fave programme starting up in the next room. What
  do you do?
  a. Get up straight away and go and watch it –
     leaving the computer on all night.
  b. Get up straight away and go and watch it –
     then come back afterwards and turn the computer off.
  c. Shut down the computer before you toddle off.

♡ 8. How often do you eat red meat?
  a. Every day.
  b. A couple of times a week.
  c. Hardly ever/never.

♡ 9. What do you do with used paper?
  a. Chuck it in the bin.
  b. Use it as scrap paper then chuck it in the bin.
  c. Use it as scrap paper then recycle it.

10. Do you use rechargeable batteries?
    a. Never, didn't know there were different kinds.
    b. Sometimes.
    c. Usually/always.

SCORES

Mostly As: You are an eco-wombat.

2

You think food grows shrink-wrapped on trees. You're totally clueless when it comes to the plight of the planet – you need to shape up, and fast! The future of the globe depends on you and your mates.

Mostly Bs: You are an eco-worrier.

2

You're concerned about our planet and you'd like to be greener, but you're not always sure what you can do. Never fear, your mates are here – this book will set you on the right path . . .

Mostly Cs: You are an eco-superhero.

6

You're a shining beacon when it comes to setting an example for green living. If more people were like you, the planet wouldn't need saving. But there is always more to do, so read on for loads of good ideas!

Ask the Expert

Eco-issues can be really confusing. For instance, if the whole planet is covered in water, why do people go on about how we need to save it all the time? Luckily, TJ's older brother Paul has a college friend who's really into all things ecological and has just got a job working for a big green campaigning organisation. So TJ asked if he could meet up with us to explain some things over a cuppa. His name is Tim. He arrived on a bike, was well fit and we are all totally in love. We renamed him Tasty Tim but would just like to point out that he is not the reason we've all converted to being green. . . but he definitely helped.

NB If you're like Nesta and just want to know what to do, skip this section and go straight to Tim's top tips for saving the planet, on page 29.

I'd just like it noted that I did stay and listen to what Timbo had to say and am not as shallow as some people make out – Nesta.

All:	Hello, Tim.
Tim:	Hello, girls.

TJ: So can you tell us, in a nutshell, why it's so important to go green?

Tim: Sure I can. The most important reason is global warming.

Nesta: *(fluttering her eyelashes enough to cause a mini-hurricane)* Why?

Tim: It causes climate change.

Nesta: *(flutter, flutter)* And why is that?

Tim: The Earth's climate naturally changes over long time periods, swinging from long Ice Ages to shorter, warmer periods. However, recently, scientific data says that the Earth is warming quickly because of human activity, rather than naturally and slowly. The ten hottest years on record have all occurred since the early 1990s –

Nesta: About the time I arrived on the planet *(breaks into song)* Feelin' hot hot hot . . .

TJ: Nesta, shut up.

Nesta: You have to admit that it is a bit of a coincidence.

Izzie: I very much doubt whether your arrival on the planet accounts for global warming – now let Tim tell us about it and stop interrupting.

Nesta: Pff. Only being friendly here, but *do* go on, Tim.

Tim: This means that species have not had time to adapt and nature can no longer cope. The polar ice caps –

Nesta: I can relate to that. *(She starts fanning herself.)* I have a hard time coping too sometimes in the presence of the opposite species.

Lucy: Ignore our friend, Tim. She has a rare illness called flirtoxia. She's taking medication for it but still has outbreaks. It's very sad. Please do go on *(glares at Nesta)*. Some of us are genuinely interested in what you're saying.

Nesta: I'm interested. I am. I *am*.

Tim: OK. Er, where was I?

TJ: Polar ice caps.

Tim: Oh right. Yes. The polar ice caps are beginning to melt, causing loss of habitat, rising sea levels and increased risk of tidal waves, flooding, loss of land and death. Hot areas have got even hotter, so there are more and more droughts, causing famine and starvation. Typhoons, hurricanes, tornadoes and other weather extremes are all now much more frequent than we've ever known before. Climate change obviously has disastrous implications for all living things on the planet. Nesta, you've gone all quiet.

Nesta: God, that is so depressing. *So* depressing. Now I'm depressed. Is there any hope for any of us?

Izzie: As well as being a major flirt, Tim, our friend here is also a drama queen.

Nesta: I am so not. I'm just misunderstood. Like that global warming thingee.

Tim: Exactly.

Nesta: I know what will cheer us up. Let's have hot chocolates with marshmallows in them and continue this conversation later.

(Five hot chocolates and five choc chip cookies later.)

Izzie: So is there a difference between the greenhouse effect and global warming?

Tim: Well, greenhouse gases are chemicals that occur naturally and form a blanket around the Earth, trapping heat that would otherwise escape into space. Carbon dioxide is the main greenhouse gas – it's a colourless, odourless gas that occurs naturally in the Earth's atmosphere.

Lucy: Oh, so that shouldn't be a problem, should it, if it's natural?

Tim: The trouble is that we have been pumping additional CO_2 . . .

Nesta: Hang on, explain CO_2?

Tim: Oh sorry, that's another way of saying carbon dioxide. Anyway, people have been pumping huge amounts of extra CO_2 into the atmosphere for the last couple of hundred years.

Izzie: Why, what happened two hundred years ago?

Tim: That's when the industrial revolution happened, when people started burning large amounts of fuel to produce energy for things like factories and transport – and that created lots of extra carbon dioxide. And ever since then, we have intensified the greenhouse effect and increased the Earth's temperature, causing global warming.

Nesta: I can feel another hot chocolate coming on. Is there any good news in all of this, or is it all bad?

Tim: It's not too late, Nesta, but people have to act now. Like another problem is that humans have been greedy, stripping the planet of resources such as oil, metals and gems which have taken millions of years to form and which can't be replaced. And then we've gone and wasted all these resources by throwing them away as waste into enormous outdoor burial pits for rubbish called landfill sites.

TJ: I know about these. There are over two thousand landfill sites in the UK and they are predicted to be full within five to ten years.

Tim: That's right, TJ. And chemicals and toxic waste leaks out from some rubbish, such as dumped fridges, and this pollutes the surrounding land.

TJ: All that doesn't sound good.

Tim: It's not.

Lucy: But isn't some rubbish biodegradable?

Tim: Some is.

Nesta: What's biodegradable?

Tim: Something that is biodegradable breaks down physically and/or chemically over time. For example, food scraps, cotton, wool and paper are biodegradable, but plastics, polyester and many other man-made items generally are not. Anything that isn't biodegradable ends up as problem waste for the planet – not just because it's generally buried in the landfill sites, which are filling up rapidly, but also because it's transported there by large lorries, burning lots of fuel and causing pollution.

Izzie: Can't we just burn it?

Tim: Burning waste isn't the answer, because burning rubbish releases pollutants into the air, including gases that contribute to climate change. The ash that is left over is often toxic and has to be disposed of in landfill sites. We need to change our attitudes towards rubbish.

TJ: Does that mean recycling?

Tim: Yes, but that's only one of the Three Rs. They're all really important.

Lucy: Three Rs? Didn't we do those in infant school?

Tim: No, these are the green Rs: Reduce, Reuse, Recycle. 'Reduce' means we should create less waste to begin with. That means only buying stuff we really need.

Izzie: And not buying things with loads of packaging?

Tim: That's right, Izzie – a lot of packaging is unnecessary. We should also avoid using disposable items if there's a good alternative available.

Izzie: What, like those coffee cups everyone carries around?

Tim: Yes, and many other products like disposable cloths, plates, cutlery, plastic bags, even cameras, which are designed to be used only once then thrown away.

That means they're not a good use of the Earth's precious materials and fuel, and they also end up on those landfill sites. So it's much better to choose things which can be used again and again. We should also repair things wherever possible, instead of replacing them.

TJ: How about 'Reuse'?

Tim: Well, yes, 'Reuse' means not throwing anything away if it could still be useful – stuff which ends up on rubbish heaps could often be reused in some way – for example, using glass jars for storage. And once an item can't be used any more in its current form, the materials it's made of can often be turned into something new – that's Recycling, and we all need to recycle as much as we can.

TJ: So really you're saying that we should think twice before we throw *anything* away?

Tim: Exactly right.

Nesta: OK, I've got a question for you. Why are we always being told that we should save water?

Tim: Well, human beings in developed
countries are demanding more and more
water – for instance, to fill our kettles,
our swimming pools and our garden water
features. So water companies have to
extract more water from existing
underground reservoirs and rivers.

Izzie: But aren't they refilled by rain?

Nesta: Yeah – we get enough of it!

Tim: Not quickly enough. That means that
too much water is drained away from the
natural habitats of wildlife, and low river
levels increase the concentration of
pollutants in the water, so there is less
oxygen for the plant and animal life there.
And you may think that oceans aren't
affected by water use in your home, but
think again. Waste water eventually finds

its way back there, and if waste water is polluted, then the seas are polluted too. So saving water saves the oceans.

Nesta: And what the heck is a carbon footprint?

Tim: Your carbon footprint is a measurement of how much carbon dioxide you produce just by going about your daily life.

Lucy: Like what we breathe out? Because we breathe out carbon dioxide, don't we? I remember doing that in science. Are you saying stop breathing?

Tim: No, Lucy, I'm not. You produce additional carbon dioxide when you travel in a car or aeroplane, put the heating on, switch on lights or boil a kettle. All those things rely on the burning of fossil fuels, which emit carbon dioxide and other greenhouse gases that contribute to global warming.

TJ: What's food got to do with going green, Tim?

Tim: A lot, TJ. Eating local produce is much better than eating stuff that's grown miles away, because all the planes and lorries which transport food use up fuel and also emit carbon dioxide. That increases greenhouse gases, which in turn increase global warming, which increases climate change. Do you know what food miles are?

TJ: It's the number of miles that food produce travels from where it's grown to where it's eaten. We did that at school.

Tim: Exactly. And food that counts for a large number of food miles not only involves more fuel usage, it also needs more protective packaging to keep it in a decent state, so it's a double whammy for the environment. You should choose local produce and less packaged food whenever you can.

Izzie: So what about organic food?

Tim: Organic food is much better for the environment because it hasn't been grown using pesticides and fertilisers, which can have long-term effects on the land and also insects and animals which eat them – including us. For instance, if veg is treated with pesticides and fertilisers, humans may be eating those too when they eat the veg.

Lucy: That's what my dad says too, which is why he sells organic veg in his shop.

Izzie: Tastes better too.

Nesta: What is fair trade, Tim? For instance, is it something I could do with your girlfriend?

Tim: Not sure she'd like that.

Nesta: Worth a try. Like with going green, all you have to do is be open to changing a few things.

Tim: *(cough)* OK. Um, not sure that's what I meant exactly. So. Yes. Fair trade. This is a movement ensuring that people in the developing world are getting a fair deal for their products and encouraging them to use environmentally-friendly methods.

Lucy: And any product that is fair trade is clearly marked so on the package, isn't that right, Tim?

Tim: That's right. Fair trade can also help another big problem – population growth. If people have a reasonable quality of life, which fair trade promotes, they tend to have fewer children. That means the population grows more slowly, which is good for the planet.

TJ: I've never properly understood what genetically-modified means. Can you explain?

Tim: Genetically modified plants have been scientifically altered to increase their yield or quality. Many people are worried about the long-term effects this will have on animals and humans.

Nesta: You mentioned fossil fuels before, Tim. Sounds like they're hot. A bit like you.

Tim: Actually I am starting to feel a bit hot.
Er, could I have a glass of water? Thanks.
So, right, can any of you tell me what the
three fossil fuels are?

Nesta: My grandpa, my grandma and my Aunt
Sadie. They really are a bunch of old
fossils.

TJ: Coal, oil and natural gas.

Nesta: Smarty pants.

Tim: You're right, TJ. We burn these to
produce energy. When they are burned,
these components mix with oxygen in the
atmosphere. The result is carbon dioxide –
which as you now know is the main
greenhouse gas, causing global warming,

which causes climate change . . . which brings us back to where we started. Um . . . can I go now?

Nesta: Just one last thing before you go – now that you have explained all the problems and made me feel totally depressed, can you say what we have to *do* to save the planet, for those of us who might have been slightly – um – *distracted* during what you just said?

Tim: OK. Here goes.

Tasty Tim's Top Ten Tips for Saving the Planet

1. Save energy: only use what you really need, and switch off anything you're not actually using – lights, heating, computers, TV.
2. Don't waste water.
3. Bin the bin – Reduce, Reuse and Recycle.
4. Walk, bike or take public transport rather than travelling by car. And don't go by aeroplane if you can avoid it.
5. Eat locally-grown, low-packaged and/or organic food whenever possible.
6. When you're shopping, only buy what you really need, reuse bags, go for products with little packaging, and choose fair trade and organic items when you can.
7. Choose greener cleaning products, or make your own.
8. Help conservation campaigns.
9. Think green when it comes to gift-giving.

10. Speak up about saving the planet! Nag your parents, teachers and mates to go greener. Email your MP.

Keep reading for loads of brilliant ideas on how to green up your act and make Tim's tips a part of your everyday life.

CHAPTER 2

Be a Green Girl

A Note from TJ

I used to want to be a writer, but I've changed my mind recently. I think that I might become a politician. I want to make my mark and do something that will make a difference. OK, I might write the occasional book because books influence the way people think too, but politicians are the ones who have the main say about change and stuff – which makes me think, how come they just sit back and let our planet go down the drain? Don't they care about people without enough water to drink, animals in danger of dying out and glaciers melting in Antarctica?

Anyway, the real point is, it's politicians who have the most power to change things, but that doesn't mean we can't do anything. Politicians need voters, and in a few years' time that will be you and me! Until then, we can talk to parents and teachers and any other adults who will listen, and make sure that they realise how crucial green issues are, so that they vote for politicians who will really act to protect the planet – not just talk about it. We can also get together and join protests and campaigns (this is a fab way to meet boys who have a bit of oomph). And if I do become a politician, you can vote for me some day!

But we can all start RIGHT NOW by taking responsibility for our own lives. How? I hear you say. Read on. We've written about all the things we think we can do to make the world a better place, and we've divided them up into three sections: Green Girl ('easy-peasy-lemon-squeezy' level), Green Queen ('bit of a challenge' level) and Green Goddess ('polish that halo' level).

So here goes with the easy-peasy stuff.

TJ X

Tasty Tim's Eco-Facts

Did you know that households in the UK produce about twenty-seven million tonnes of rubbish each year? That's about the weight of 2.7 million dinosaurs! Keep reading to find out how a lot of that rubbish could be put to good use.

Top Turn-Offs to Save the Planet

Our biggest turn-offs used to be greasy hair, B.O. and boys who acted like they knew it all. But now we think about turn-offs in a very different way. Every time you use an electrical gadget in your house you're using electricity – which comes from burning fossil fuels – which pumps out greenhouse gases into the atmosphere – which contributes to climate change – which will wreak havoc on the environment and destroy living things and could lead to the end of the planet. And you may not know this, but leaving electrical equipment on standby uses almost as much electricity as

when you're actually using it. Aaargh! However, there's a simple solution. Turn things off! *(Yay. Tick. Can do. Off goes my computer for a start when I'm not using it – I used to leave it on standby – Lucy)*

SOME EASY CAN-DOS

1 If you have a radio alarm that's mains operated, flick it off at the plug every morning – it'll take you only a few extra seconds to reset it at night.
2 Turn your DVD player, CD player, Nintendo Wii player etc. off at the wall socket (or unplug it) when you're not using it.
3 When you're watching TV, don't have all the lights blazing in the room at the same time.
4 When your programme's finished, don't leave the telly on in the background – make the break and turn it off instead.
5 Don't use the remote to put the set onto standby – actually walk across the room and

turn it off properly. *(As a bonus, you'll burn off a bit of the chocolate you've probably just noshed back in front of the box too. Only a couple of calories – but it all adds up, doesn't it?– Izzie.)*

6 Unplug your mobile charger as soon as your phone's juiced up. Whatever you do, don't leave it charging overnight.

7 Make it a habit to turn off the light when you leave a room – unless someone's still in there, of course . . . *(Though it's quite a laugh to turn off the light in the loo when your brother's in there – Lucy.)*

TOP TIPS FOR GREEN GIRLS

Go around your house and count how many lightbulbs you have. How many of these are energy-saving lightbulbs? If you replace normal lightbulbs with energy-saving ones, your family won't just be saving the planet, they'll be saving money on their electricity bill too.

Tasty Tim's Eco-Facts

Did you know that a colour TV left on standby can use eighty-five per cent of the energy it uses when it's actually on? And in the UK, out of all the energy used by mobile phones, a whopping ninety-five per cent is wasted energy because of chargers being left plugged in when the phone's actually finished charging. So switch things off when they're not in use and be instantly greener!

Quick Fix

A wind-up alarm clock is a fantastic green alternative to one that runs on mains electricity or batteries.

Green Up Your Computer

If you're anything like us, you spend a-g-e-s on your computer every day. What with Facebook and MySpace and homework and coursework and

Facebook and emailing mates and checking your online horoscope and Facebook and chat rooms and blogging and – oh, yes, did we mention Facebook? While computers are great for cutting down on paper (for instance, you can get your celeb gossip online rather than having to buy a magazine) they're not good when it comes to electricity usage. So here are our top green tips for being cuter when you use your computer.

1　Position your computer near a window if possible, so you can do your homework in natural light as often as you can rather than needing to turn the light on. *(It's better for your overall energy flow to be in natural than artificial light anyway – Izzie.)*

2　Try to ration your computer-usage to cut down on electricity. Do you really need to spend that

long in a chat room? Try to allocate one day every week to be computer-free.

3 Think twice before you use your computer printer – only use it when it's really necessary, because laser printers release ozone into the environment, as well as eating up paper.

4 When you're printing, set your printer to the 'quick print' option, so you use less ink.

5 Always print on both sides of your paper.

6 Put a box next to your computer so you can collect any printouts you don't need for recycling.

7 Don't leave your computer on standby when your mates phone up for a chat – use the 'sleep' function (which can reduce energy wastage by sixty-five per cent) or, even better, turn it off altogether.

Tasty Tim's Eco-Facts

The average temperature in Western Siberia has increased by 3°C in the last forty years. That means huge amounts of ice melt, which raises river and ocean levels and causes flooding, which means that animals which like cold places have fewer places to live. It's caused by global warming – which is why we all have to act now.

TOP TIPS FOR GREEN GIRLS

Don't send an old-but-
still-working computer to the
rubbish tip just because it's
out-of-date and you're lucky
enough to have landed a new
one. Someone else might be
glad of it, so try offering it to a
school or community centre or a
local charity (ring up and check
beforehand if they accept electrical
items). If your old computer is bust,
rather than dumping it, a computer company might be
glad of it to use as spare parts. If you really do have to
bin it, make sure you take it to your local rubbish and
recycling centre so it's disposed of in the right way,
because computers contain chemicals that are
dangerous if they leak into the soil.

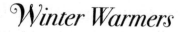
Winter Warmers

Ahh, winter! The season of sleigh bells, Santa, Jack Frost nipping at your nose – and burning loads and loads of fossil fuels to try to keep warm! Very eco-friendly – NOT. Here's how to stay green *and* cosy . . .

1   When the weather gets cold and wintry, spend an afternoon with your mates making draught excluders – sealing up gaps is one of the cheapest and easiest ways to reduce heat-loss. You don't have to make those hideous snake ones that always end up at jumble sales. See who can create the funkiest draught excluder for the bottom of their bedroom door – decorate them with bits of fake fur, feather boa, sequins, ribbons and buttons (all recycled from old clothes, of course!).

2 During the day, don't head straight to turn on the fire or the central heating. Instead, put on some warmer clothes. You don't have to sit there looking like Queen Nerd from Nerdville. Invest in a gorgeous snuggly jumper and a pair of fluffy slippers, and if the cute boy you fancy pops round, use the cold weather as an excuse to snuggle up close under a sofa throw – that way, you'll be saving body heat and saving the planet at the same time. *(Now you're talking. Count me in. I think I'm really beginning to get this green thing – Nesta.)*

3 Resist the charms of an electric blanket at night – take a hot water bottle to bed instead, or pull on a pair of bedsocks (don't think Marge Simpson, aim for Meg Ryan in *Sleepless in Seattle*).

Quick Fix

When you're boiling a kettle to make a cup of whatever, don't fill it to the brim – only heat as much water as you need. And make sure you don't go wandering off while it's heating up, so you have to re-boil it again two minutes later! (Oops, that's so me – TJ.)

Be a Green Girl

Tasty Tim's Eco-Facts

It takes twenty times more raw materials to raise animals for meat than it does to grow grains, fruit and vegetables. It's simple – if you want to be greener, eat less meat!

Be a Natural Beauty

OK, so we all want to look and feel our best. But did you know that some beauty products are damaging the planet? 'Duh, how can a bit of lip gloss damage the planet?' we hear you say. Well, for a start, beauty products are some of the most over-packaged items in shops. And make-up and perfume are often packed with chemicals and synthetic ingredients that need a lot of factory processing. In Europe and the USA, a cosmetic or fragrance product can call itself 'natural' even if only one per cent of its ingredients fall into that category.

100% girlie stuff

But never fear. All is not lost. There are ways we can be green and gorgeous.

1 Go for eco-friendly beauty companies. For instance, The Body Shop was one of the first companies to promote eco-awareness and they are continually campaigning on the issues of environmental awareness, climate change and safe drinking water.

2 Choose shop-bought products with care. As a general rule, products with fewer ingredients are greener than products with a loooooong list of ingredients, plant-based products take a lot less manufacturing than petroleum-based products, and bath salts contain fewer chemicals than bubble baths.

3 Reduce your use of shop-bought products altogether. For instance, when you're choosing make-up, go for brands that are refillable, like MAC. You'll waste far fewer containers and it'll

be cheaper in the long run too. Even better, make your own – see below for some brilliant ideas.

4   When it comes to shampoo and conditioner, most of us use far more than we actually need. Shampoo once instead of twice and see if you can spot the difference. Bet your hair's just as glossy and gorgeous.

5   Reduce your use of disposable beauty products, like make-up remover wipes. A facial wash does the same job but without as much waste.

6   Um, not exactly beauty, but organic sanitary towels or tampons are better for the environment than the ordinary kind – and probably better for you too!

ƊIY: Natural Indulgence!

Instead of buying highly processed and packaged fragrances from shops, you can make divine scents at home by mixing two or three drops of essential oils such as jasmine, rose and neroli into an unscented base oil like grapeseed, almond or sunflower.

You can use essential oils in unscented base oils in all sorts of other ways – for skin moisturisers, as bath oils, and as hair rinses to give your hair that extra shine. There's a bewildering variety to suit different skin and hair types, so ask for advice – unless you're like Izzie and you know all about essential oils already because natural remedies are your thing.

Be like Lucy and experiment with making your own luscious beauty products from natural ingredients like avocado, honey, oatmeal, banana and egg. Trying out natural recipes is a great excuse to get together with your mates for a girls-only evening of pampering, chatting and relaxing. Turn the page for some scrummy examples.

Kiwi Facial Cleanser

Ingredients (makes one application):

1 kiwi fruit
2 tablespoons plain yogurt
1 tablespoon orange water
1 tablespoon apricot or almond oil
1 tablespoon honey
1 teaspoon finely ground almonds
2 drops orange (or your favourite citrus) essential oil

Instructions:

Purée the kiwi fruit in a food processor until liquid. Add the yogurt, orange water, almond or apricot oil, honey and ground almonds and process until thick and creamy. Add the essential oil and stir to mix. Massage gently over face and neck to cleanse. Rinse well.

Zingy Ginger Skin Cream

Ingredients:

5 cm piece fresh ginger
2 teaspoons light sesame oil
2 teaspoons apricot kernel oil
2 teaspoons vitamin E oil
$\frac{1}{2}$ cup cocoa butter

Instructions:

Preheat oven on lowest setting. Finely grate the ginger, then squeeze this over a small bowl to extract the juice. Place the ingredients (including the ginger juice) in an overproof dish and put in the oven until the cocoa butter is melted and the oils are blended. Allow to cool, then pour into a clean, dry container and store in a cool dry place. You can also add a couple of drops of orange or another essential oil.

Cucumber Hair Treat

Ingredients:

1 egg
4 tablespoons olive oil
$\frac{1}{4}$ cucumber, peeled

Instructions:

Blend the egg, olive oil and cucumber. Spread evenly through your hair, leave on for ten minutes, then rinse thoroughly. For best results, do this once a month.

Strawberry Hand and Foot Smoother

Ingredients:

8-10 strawberries
2 tablespoons apricot or olive oil
1 teaspoon coarse salt, such as sea salt

Instructions:

Mix together all ingredients, massage gently into hands and feet, rinse and pat dry.

Luscious Rose Bath Milk

Ingredients:

1 cup rose petals OR $\frac{1}{2}$ cup rose water
(available from health food stores)
$\frac{1}{2}$ cup coconut milk

Instructions:

Add the rose petals or rose water and coconut milk to a
warm bath and relax.

Divine, and they make fab presents for birthdays
and Christmas too.

Quick Fix

*Get up and move more! If you feel good inside,
you'll look great on the outside. Skin looks
glowing and eyes look bright and sparkly if you're
into exercise. Walk to school or get on your bike,
instead of getting a lift in the car. Save your
money, your waistline and the environment all in
one go. Even if you only step it out or use pedal
power three times a week, your metabolism will
quicken, you'll stay in trim, you'll have more
energy – and there'll be less pollution.*

Tasty Tim's Eco-Facts

Ninety-five per cent of the fruit and fifty per cent of the vegetables eaten in the UK are imported. That means a lot of trucks, trains and planes putting out planet-poisoning fumes to get them to a shop near you. Read on to find out what to do.

Eco-Friendly Food Shopping

It can be very frustrating not to be in control of what type of food ends up in your house. For instance, Lucy's parents always buy organic healthy fruit and veg, although she often just craves a burger. *(Oi, no need to tell everyone! – Lucy)* Izzie's mum used to buy fast food, until Izzie told her that what she really wanted was organic healthy fruit and veg. *(My body is my temple . . . plus I have to think of my hips. Groan – Izzie)*

Here are a few ways you can have more influence:

❀ Offer to help with the weekly shop.

❀ Suggest that it would be easier to get everything in one big shop rather than several little ones – using the car less means saving in petrol usage and in carbon dioxide emissions.

❀ Remind your parents that it's a good idea to buy essential items in bulk, which again means fewer trips to the shops in the car and also means less packaging (plus often it's cheaper).

And if you're on the spot, you'll be able to persuade whoever does the shopping to follow some go-greener guidelines,

1 Buy locally-grown produce – compared to produce from miles away overseas, local food needs less transport, which means less petrol and less carbon dioxide. Locally-grown produce also has less packaging than produce from far away. Always check labels to see where food has come from.

2 Buy fruit and veg that are in season (meaning the time of year they naturally grow) – this will have involved less use of chemical fertilisers and they will probably have been grown locally too. To find out which foods are in season each month, look at www.bbc.co.uk/food/ in_season/.

3 Buy organic fruit and vegetables – because they're grown without pesticides, they're less damaging for the environment (and probably less damaging for us as well). They taste better too.

4 Avoid genetically-modified products – the long-term consequences for the environment are not yet known and could be harmful. Food that is genetically-modified should always say so on the label.

Be a Green Girl

5 Buy fair trade products – these are products which guarantee that farmers and employees have been treated and paid fairly, and that they've been made in ways that are environmentally-friendly. A fair trade product will always say so on the label.

6 Take your old plastic bags with you so you don't have to grab new ones at the supermarket, or buy a 'bag for life' which you can use every time.

7 Lastly, check out your local supermarket's recycling facilities and don't forget to take along recyclable stuff that isn't collected from your house.

Tasty Tim's Eco-Facts

Plastic bags begin life as petrochemicals, which go through umpteen energy-eating processes before they are transformed into carriers. In one year alone in the UK we use enough plastic bags to cover the whole of London! Always take your own bag with you when you go shopping.

Quick Fix

It's better for the environment to choose vegetarian rather than meat-based meals, because meat production requires far more energy than eating locally-produced fruit, vegetables, grains and pulses. This doesn't mean that you have to give up scrummy weekend bacon butties or say no to your mum's famous lasagne – but try to go for the veggie option more often. And when you eat fish, try to steer clear of endangered species. (Check out www.fishonline.org/advice/eat for which fish are OK to eat.)

Be a Green Girl

TOP TIPS FOR GREEN GIRLS

Find out if you have a local farm
shop or farmers' market where
you can buy local produce.
Your family's food will be
fresher and if you bike there,
it will be cutting down on
environmental pollution and
energy use as well. Some farm
shops have bottle refilling
schemes too (for things like olive
oil, vinegar etc), which is a brilliant
way to recycle.

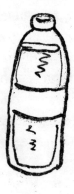

Wonderful Water

Without water, there would be no life on Earth.
Although most of the water on the planet is
undrinkable salt water in the seas and oceans, it is
still an essential part of our eco-system, which we
are polluting with toxic waste. Also, hot areas
which are already short of drinking water are
becoming even drier, due to climate change. In
many parts of the world which have plenty of fresh
water, climate change is causing frequent flooding,
contaminating the existing water supply. So make
sure you treat water like the precious resource it is.

1 If you love a deep bath, try to ration yourself to
wallowing in just one long soak per week. Try a
shower instead – it uses MUCH less water and
you'll be just as clean. But don't spend ages
under one of those supersonic power showers
with a million jets and nozzles, or you'll use
more than a bath!

2 Turn off the tap while you brush your teeth –
by leaving the tap on while you perfect your
smile, you can waste
up to four and a half
litres of water.

3 We all know that to have sparkly eyes and glowing skin, we should drink lots of water every day. But you can help the environment if you don't go for bottled waters – just drink tap water (buy a water filter jug if you prefer the taste). By not buying bottles all the time, you're cutting down on both manufacturing and waste – and you're saving money too.

4 If you like drinking ice-cold water, instead of running the tap until the water gets cold enough, fill a bottle and store it in the fridge.

5 Stop anyone in your family from adding to water pollution by getting rid of liquids like oil or paint down drains or sinks. There are special facilities at rubbish and recycling centres to dispose of these without contaminating our water supplies.

Tasty Tim's Eco-Facts

By the year 2025, it is estimated that two-thirds of the world's population will face a water shortage. Make sure you don't waste a drop.

TOP TIPS FOR GREEN GIRLS

The production of shop-bought fruit juices takes both huge amounts of packaging and huge amounts of water – about twenty-two glasses of water are used in processing just one glass of orange juice. If you buy a juicer and make your own juices at home, you'll be helping the environment in the long term. Alternatively, just eat fruit! You'll be saving water, saving energy, saving food miles, and saving on packaging ending up in landfill.

Tasty Tim's Eco-Facts

People in the UK buy twelve billion drinks cans every year – enough to stretch to the moon and back – but only a quarter are recycled. The energy saved by recycling just one can is enough to run a TV set for three hours!

Quick Fix

Start a trend at your school to use refillable pens (like fountain pens) rather than disposable biros. Refillable pens may cost more to start off with – but you'll be cutting down on the energy used to make disposable ones, to transport them to the shops for sale, and then to get rid of them when they're empty. If you choose refillable pens in funky designs, you'll probably find that they'll catch on you'll all be trendsetters, and everyone else will soon have them without even realising that they're an eco-friendly choice. Result.

TOP TIPS FOR GREEN GIRLS

Gyms and leisure centres use loads of energy for lighting and heating and powering equipment, so the greenest way to get fit is to exercise outdoors. It's also better for your heart and soul (seriously, research has shown that exercising outdoors

benefits your state of mind and your heartbeat more than doing the same thing indoors). You could try things like:

❀ cycling *(But don't wear cycling shorts – a big fashion no-no – Lucy.)*

❀ jogging *(Get real – Nesta.)*

❀ horse-riding outdoors *(That's more like it: stylish clothes and fit stable-boys – Nesta.)*

Go Wild in the Country

If you're feeling blue, there's nothing like some sunshine and fresh air to clear the cobwebs away, put a spring back into your step and a smile back onto your face. Izzie swears that getting outside into nature helps you deepen your connection to Planet Earth and become filled with a sense of peace and harmony. *(That's if your pants aren't filled with ants first – Nesta.)* There are a few easy dos and don'ts so you can be eco-friendly when you're dog-walking, or throwing a picnic for your mates, or meandering through a meadow trying to commune with nature, or strolling through a park arm-in-arm with Mr Cutenik. *(Now you're talking – Nesta.)*

1   Don't pick wild flowers – they often don't grow back, so this can lead to loss of habitat.
2   Do take home any food containers, bags or wrappers – not just because litter looks rubbish *(litter looks rubbish, geddit?)*, but because wild animals might think that the scent of them is actually food itself, and of course, if they eat these things they can become very ill or even die. They might also pose a tangling or suffocation risk.
3   If you're walking the dog, make sure you keep it under control, so it doesn't disturb wild birds and other animals.

Tasty Tim's Eco-Facts

Each year, one million sea birds, 100,000 marine mammals, and 50,000 fur seals are killed as a result of eating or being strangled by plastic, including sandwich bags and Styrofoam cups. Try to cut down on your use of these things.

Stop Wasting Paper

Did you know that it takes twenty-eight per cent less energy to recycle paper than to produce paper from scratch? So you can help save the planet if you use paper recycling schemes, which are available at supermarkets and on street corners. But there are other ways to make paper go further:

1 Buy paper with at least thirty per cent recycled content in it in the first place.
2 Write on both sides of the paper and then recycle it again afterwards.
3 Make it your job at home to save paper, as well as recycle it. Sort through envelopes to see if there are any that can be used again to post things, or reused as scrap paper for shopping lists etc.

4 Don't print out anything from a computer unless you're sure you need to.

Tasty Tim's Eco-Facts

It's estimated that every person in the UK throws away on average two trees' worth of paper and card every year. It's so easy to recycle paper, make sure you don't waste a scrap.

Quick Fix

Whenever you get a swanky paper bag from a posh shop instead of a plastic carrier, reuse it for shopping or to carry stuff to school. Of course, this last tip is for the sake of fashion, as well as for saving the planet. After all, what would you rather look like – a bag lady or a boutique lady?!

Give Green Gifts

How many times have you struggled to think of a really good present for someone on their birthday or at Christmas? If you go green, you'll be able to stun your mates and your family with some truly fab, fun, unusual gifts, while helping to save the planet at the same time.

Remember, it may be the thought that counts, but if you're going to give someone a material gift, try to find something they're going to use, otherwise it can be a waste of your time, money and the planet's resources. If you give green consumables – such as organic teas, fair trade coffee, organic biscuits etc. – your family or friends will enjoy them all the more because they can tuck in with a clear conscience! If you choose gifts that are grown or made locally, this will save the environment from emissions created by transporting them from miles away. And don't forget about vintage gifts – you'll be able to afford higher-quality items second-hand than if you were thinking of buying them new, and it's a form of recycling too.

Here are a few of our ideas for some of the green gifts we'd love to give or get ourselves . . .

Be a Green Girl

Top Ten Eco-Gifts

1 Fair trade chocs.
2 Essential oils and aromatherapy products.
3 Toiletry lotions and potions made from natural, organic products. *(It's even better if you make these yourself – Lucy.)*
4 Natural, beeswax candles.
5 Live, growing pot plants instead of cut flowers.
6 Packets of seeds – especially vegetables or wildflowers to grow. *(Are you joking? Like, a packet of parsnips? – Nesta. OK, We'll give you broccoli then – Lucy. Yeah, just because you don't want them, it doesn't mean other people won't appreciate them – TJ. OK, let them have them then. Don't ever let it be said that I am stingy – Nesta.)*
7 Anything rechargeable. *(We've heard of a mobile phone recharger that works by pedal power while you're riding your bike – how cool is that? – TJ.)*

64

8 Anything made from recycled materials.
   (I've seen some fab jewellery made from recycled glass – Lucy.)
9 Anything made from organic materials.
   (A snuggly organic cotton bathrobe would do me nicely – Nesta.)
10 Carbon-neutral CDs *(More and more artists are releasing these, including Massive Attack, Coldplay, Foo Fighters, Feeder and Sting.)*

Give a Promise

(this is our fave green pressie idea)

A great green gift is to make 'promise' vouchers for your mates, mum and dad, or brothers and sisters for things like:

❀ one breakfast in bed
❀ one babysitting session
❀ one manicure
❀ one pedicure
❀ one massage
❀ a make-up makeover
❀ a hair makeover

❀ an entire evening of pampering

❀ a picnic in the park

❀ an all-expenses-paid trip to the movies

❀ one romantic meal for two

❀ one car wash

❀ one lawn-mowing session

❀ a week of dog-walking

❀ a week of washing up

❀ a week of loading and unloading the dishwasher

❀ a week of hanging out the washing

❀ a week of ironing

❀ a week of hoovering

❀ a month of watering the plants

❀ a month of pet-feeding and cleaning-out

❀ a month of giving help with homework

❀ a promise to lend your fave jacket/bag/ dress/shoes on one special occasion

❀ a promise to keep your bedroom tidy for eternity *(Hang on, now that's going a bit far . . . Izzie.)*

Green Group Giving

These things are a bit pricey for you to buy on your own, but if you can club together with a couple of other people, they'd make great green presents:

1 iPod solar charger
2 solar-powered outdoor lanterns or a water feature
3 theatre or concert tickets (a pair – after all, who wants to go on their own?)
4 membership of a zoo or aquarium that has a conservation programme
5 membership of a museum or gallery (if you see a nice-looking boy roaming about, he might be brainy as well as buff)
6 a tree (if it's not possible to give the person an actual tree to plant, there are lots of organisations who undertake tree planting)
7 the adoption of an endangered wild animal or sponsorship of an animal at a zoo or aquarium that does conservation work

8 give a goat! Or another gift from a charity such as the Oxfam Unwrapped selection (see www.oxfam.org.uk/shop) and World Vision (see www.greatgifts.org), where you choose a present such as school textbooks, seeds or vaccinations for people who need them. The person you buy the gift for gets a greetings card with details of what you've selected in their name. All the gifts make a huge difference.

Wrap It Up!

When it comes to wrapping up your perfect pressies, don't forget to buy recycled wrapping paper, and try to use it again, or recycle it again. For mates, you can always make your own wrapping paper from pages in unwanted magazines that have pictures of their fave celebs on. Imagine a present wrapped entirely in pics of Cristiano Ronaldo – swoonsome (almost better than the pressie itself, surely)!

And at Christmas and birthdays, instead of ripping paper off gifts, take it off carefully, roll and stash it for when you need to wrap a present yourself. We have one piece of silver and white paper which has

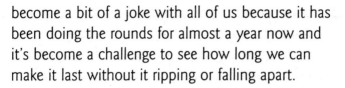

become a bit of a joke with all of us because it has been doing the rounds for almost a year now and it's become a challenge to see how long we can make it last without it ripping or falling apart.

Eco-friendly Cards

Thousands and thousands of trees are chopped down every year to make birthday and Christmas cards. Here's how to be greener when it comes to greetings:

1 Find a website that allows you to choose and send an e-card. They often have music as well as pictures, so they're a great alternative to traditional paper cards. Alternatively, use your computer to design your own card, and then email it rather than printing it out. You'll not only be saving on paper, you'll also be saving

on the fuel the post office would have used to deliver your card.

2 Get together in a group to send a card, such as asking everyone in your class to sign a single birthday card, or getting everyone in your family to send someone one joint card instead of individual ones.

3 Get creative and make your cards. Try to use recycled paper, use bits of old cards or paint and draw your own images. (Lucy is particularly good at this, being the arty one, but Nesta has a good eye for choosing bits of old mags to use for collage-effect-type cards.)

4 Deliver it yourself by foot or bike (but not if you live in England and the recipient lives in Canada – that would be a bit extreme).

5 Recycle your cards when you've finished with them. Some shops have collection points for old Christmas cards.

Quick Fix

Save money and go greener by sharing magazines with your mates. Instead of all buying copies of the same magazines every week or month, decide which ones you want, agree to buy a different mag each and then swap them round between you.

Tasty Tim's Eco-Facts

In 2008, the Woodland Trust collected over 70 million used Christmas cards for recycling. This prevented over 1400 tonnes of cards being dumped on landfill and nearly 2000 tonnes of carbon dioxide being released into the atmosphere. It also raised money for the Woodland Trust to plant 17,000 new trees in the UK. You can find out more at woodland-trust.org.uk.

Green Girl Goals

Right, you've got to the end of the chapter – well done. Now comes the interesting bit – where you stop reading and decide to DO something. We hope you'll do everything we've suggested, but you've got to start somewhere – so, flick back through the chapter and choose what you're going to do first. Have a look at our green goals and then write your own!

Green things we are going to do TODAY:

Nesta: Turn the TV off at the socket instead of leaving it on standby.

Lucy: Turn off the tap while I'm cleaning my teeth.

TJ: Offer to help with the big food shop.

Izzie: Ask Mum if we can replace our ordinary lightbulbs with energy-saving ones.

Green things we are going to start doing
THIS WEEK:

Izzie: Try making my own beauty products.

Lucy: Make a birthday card to give my dad.

Nesta: Dig out the juicer and make gorgeous juices.

TJ: Have showers instead of baths.

Now it's your turn!

Three green things I am going to do TODAY:

1 .... ☆

2 .... ☆

3 .... ☆

Five green things I am going to start doing
THIS WEEK:

1 .... ☆

2 .... ☆

3 .... ☆

4 .... ☆

5 .... ☆

CHAPTER 3

Be a Green Queen

A Note from Lucy

Hi, it's Lucy again. I hope you're getting into being a green teen by now. For me, I hadn't realised that it was going to be so do-able as well as fun. This chapter includes my fave parts – the clothes and DVD swapping. It makes such good sense to share what we have and anyone who has read the *Mates, Dates* books will already know that I love searching for vintage clothing to use in my clothes design – I just never realised that I was being green at the same time!

So if you've read the last chapter and already made some changes to your life, you're officially a groovy Green Girl – go you! Now it's time to pull out a few more stops and find out how to be a Queen of Green.

Lucy X

What – there's more? Groan –- Nesta.
Nesta, shut up – Lucy.

Tasty Tim's Eco-Facts

Eighty-four per cent of a typical household's waste can be recycled.

Rev Up Your Recycling

Recycling is soooo important because we're stripping the planet of its resources faster than they can be replaced. So once things like oil, coal, natural gas and metals are gone, they're gone. That's it – no more – zip, zero, *nada*. It's up to us to recycle what we've got, or face doing without in the future . . .

People often think that recycling is dirty and a faff but nearly everyone can recycle more – it's just a matter of wanting to. Here are our recycling rules . . .

1 Don't rely on anyone else to do it.
2 Contact your local council to find out which materials are recycled in your area, and whether they are collected or if you have to take them to a collection point. You can also find out where your nearest recycling centre is by going to

www.recycle-more.co.uk. More and more areas also have local recycling schemes you can join where you're provided with boxes and all your recycling is collected once a week or once a fortnight.

3 Ask your mum or dad if you can get a recycling bin with separate sections for different types of waste, or set up separate bins for different types of waste (e.g. paper/cardboard, glass, metals, plastic, compost, electricals, clothes, books etc.).

4 Write a list of all the items your family could recycle from now on and stick it up near the recycling bin/s.

5 Take charge of putting out each type of waste on collection day, or taking it to your local recycling banks.

$\mathcal{M}$ake the Most of Your Mobile

Whenever you, your family or your mates want to update their old, boring mobile phone to a flashy new model, stop and think. Do you really need a new one just yet or can you hang on for a while longer, and avoid contributing to all the pollution caused by manufacturing processes and transportation. Surely you can sacrifice having an all-singing all-dancing new model for the sake of the planet? *(Aaargh, if I must – Nesta.)*

❀ If you have to change your mobile phone, don't just bin it. Mobile phones contain potentially hazardous materials which can seep out when they're dumped into landfill sites and left to rot, damaging the environment.

❀ There are hundreds of companies who will gladly rescue sad, cast-out mobile phones from a life of retirement and whisk them away to developing countries, where people are hugely glad of them.

❀ Many mobile phone retail outlets will accept old models and accessories for recycling, and there are also hundreds of charities and community groups who collect old phones to recycle them in order to raise funds for their cause.

❅ You can find out the simplest way for you to recycle your old phones at www.fonebak.com.

My mum had an old Nokia mobile that we used to laugh at because it was almost prehistoric, and then a famous fashion journalist wrote an article about the very same phone and how it had become a collector's item and it was vintage. Now Mum uses her old phone with pride – Lucy.

TOP TIPS FOR GREEN QUEENS

Make sure you, your family and your mates aren't throwing away your computer ink cartridges. Some shops will refill empty cartridges for a fraction of the price of new ones, so you'll be saving money as well as the planet. Or if you log on to www.cartridgesave.co.uk, go to the recycling page and fill in your details, Cartridge Save will send you a bag in which to post back your old cartridges to them. It's freepost and it's easy. And for every cartridge recycled, a donation is made to The David Sheldrick Wildlife Trust, a charity working for the rescue and rehabilitation back into the wild of orphans of many species, particularly rhinos and elephants. *An easy-peasy one. Huzzah – Nesta.*

Quick Fix

If you meet your mates at a local coffee shop, try to choose fair trade and/or organic coffee. If your favourite café doesn't give you the option, ask if they can put these items on their menu.

Tasty Tim's Eco-Facts

Every year we fill space equivalent to 28,450 football pitches with rubbish. Land is running out! So keep thinking: Reduce, Reuse, Recycle.

Go Vintage (from Lucy)

Not so long ago, clothes that were bought from charity shops or jumble sales were called 'second-hand'. Now they're called 'vintage'. All the stars do it – well, maybe not the stars themselves, but their personal stylists certainly do. They're all out there, scouring 'vintage clothing boutiques' (read Oxfam and the local hospice shop), fighting each other over stylish dresses, funky casuals, show-stopping shoes and glamorous handbags. So why not join them – and me? I've found some fabola things, and, by recycling clothes like this, you'll be saving energy and chemicals used in manufacturing processes and helping to cut down on the planet's pollution from factories, as well as bagging a bargain. There's nothing like the feeling of chancing upon a fab bit of fabric, a great shoe *(Just the one? I think not – unless you're Prince*

Charming – Nesta), a hot handbag – and knowing that you can guarantee when you go out no one else will be wearing the same thing! Going for a rummage for vintage clothes is one of my very fave ways of spending time. Look for slip dresses to wear over your jeans, retro T-shirts, parkas, beanies, vintage dresses, cut-price designer wear, cheap V-necks – and that's just for starters. As if the low prices and prize finds weren't enough, you're also giving money to good causes so you get double the feel-good factor.

Quick Fix

It's tempting to buy clothes at rock-bottom prices, but often these fall apart in a few weeks. As well as being un-green, they're usually made by poor people who work in terrible conditions for very low wages. So decide that you'll buy two good tops which will look gorgeous all year, instead of ten cheap ones which will look awful after a couple of washes.

Hold a Clothes-Swapping Party

style arsenal

A great way that you and your mates can do more to save the planet is to pool your resources – just because you've had enough of certain possessions, it doesn't mean that they're no good to your mates. Hold a clothes-swapping party two or three times a year, when your mates bring all the clothes they're definitely not going to wear any more. Lay on a few nibbles and some music, and have a laugh trying stuff on. It's amazing how what looks rubbish on one person can look a million dollars on another! As well as having a good night, you'll all be able to add some new interest to your wardrobe for the season without outlaying any dosh at all – and you'll be helping the environment at the same time by avoiding manufacturing.

TOP TIPS FOR GREEN QUEENS

When it comes to saving the planet, dry-cleaning is bad news. Dry-cleaners use chemicals rather than water to get out stains, which react with gases in the atmosphere to form a brownish haze, polluting the skies. On top of this, one dry-cleaning chemical can cause cancer in animals. And if that wasn't bad enough, just think about all the plastic bags and metal hangers dry-cleaners use, which is really wasteful! So next time you're thinking of buying something with *Dry clean only* on the label, think of the planet and choose one you can wash at home.

Quick Fix

A lot of waste is caused by people buying stuff they don't really need. So make sure you and your mates don't spend all your free time at the shops – plan something fun like swimming or bowling instead.

DIY: Customise Your Clothes

Lucy again – one of my fave things is taking cast-off clothes and transforming them into fab new outfits. It's easy – with a bit of innovation, anyone can give old clothes a totally new look. I invested in a sewing machine a while back, because customising vintage clothes has become my main hobby – in fact I'm sure you'll see the LL label (Lucy Lovering designs) in the shops one of these days. In the meantime, here are some of my ideas for creating your own unique clothes from second-hand stuff that will beat the high street fashions hands down:

1 Add a second-hand belt to an outfit for instant impact.
2 Add material to turn a pelmet-style super-mini skirt into a boho long one.
3 Cut a frumpy long skirt into a sassy short one.

4 Shorten long trousers into cropped styles

5 Mix and (mis)match old and new styles – for instance, take a prom dress and add Gothic accessories for a funky new twist.

6 Mix and (mis)match fabrics, such as teaming tartan with polkadots, to breathe new life into old fashions.

7 For jeans, try cutting off waistbands, fraying pockets, adding iron-on transfers or gems, or getting rid of the legs and adding a ra-ra bottom.

8 Cut fabric to create bold angles and lines – for instance, changing the hemline or neckline of a plain black dress can make it appear much more fashionable and fun.

9 Add or change details such as:

- buttons
- fake fur
- lace
- fabric paint
- rhinestones

- beads
- sequins
- iron-on transfers
- fabric appliqués

10 Customise bags by adding any wild accessories
you can lay your hands on, such as earrings,
hairclips, patches, badges, studs, buttons,
tassels, dangly strings of beads etc.

*For a really unique look, wear all of the above at
once – Nesta.*

*Nesta, I think it's time you took your medication –
Lucy.*

What, what? I was just getting into it – Nesta.

Then don't – Lucy.

A girl can't win – Nesta.

TOP TIPS FOR GREEN QUEENS

When you *do* buy new clothes,
go for eco-friendly fabrics.

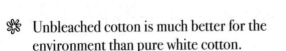

❋ Choose organic cotton if
you possibly can, because
non-organic cotton plants
are treated with enormous
amounts of pesticides and
fertilisers, which also
damage the health of cotton
pickers, who are often
young women like us. Some
high street shops are now stocking
organic T-shirts and jeans at reasonable prices.

❋ Unbleached cotton is much better for the
environment than pure white cotton.

❋ Rayon is a good choice for clothes because it's
made from trees and plants, so it involves fewer
manufacturing processes to make it.

❋ Try to avoid buying non-iron items, because even
though they're great for saving time and effort,
they're probably treated with formaldehyde, which
is poisonous to many living things.

❊ Silk is a dodgy fabric when it comes to planet-saving, because many chemicals are used during its manufacture.

Green Room Makeovers

When you and your mates want to makeover your bedrooms, you can have some great days out while helping to save the planet too. Look in charity shops, car boot sales and salvage yards for room accessories such as lampshades, cushion covers, rugs, vases and picture frames etc. People get rid of all sorts of really good quality stuff at give-away prices, especially in the posh areas of town. It's just a matter of rooting it out – and that's where mates come in handy to help. A long hard search is a great excuse to relax over a cappuccino and a muffin afterwards too. Here are some of our fave interior design themes, to get you thinking of ideas:

❊ Bollywood

❊ 1960s

❊ pink (there are many, many different shades)

* goth (black and red or purple)

* cool blues and greens

* Morocco

* your fave film

* Far East (Chinese/Japanese)

* rock 'n' roll

* different textures (e.g. silky, furry, wool, suede)

* French boudoir (lots of white, gold, pastels and glass)

* African

Quick Fix

Start a CD and DVD exchange with your mates. You'll be able to hear and watch a lot more music and movies – while feeling ecologically smug at the same time. (Of course you can be even greener by buying them second-hand in the first place, from charity shops or online stores.)

Be Green in the Garden

If you have a garden, whether it's a small patch of mud and weeds, or a sweeping lawn with overflowing flowerbeds and shrub borders, you have the scope to help the planet. It's not about aspiring to win a prize at the Chelsea Flower Show, it's all about connecting with nature and encouraging your garden wildlife. This doesn't mean that you have to help moles dig holes and go out cheering on squirrels. The countryside is changing and disappearing, so many creatures and plants out there are having a hard time surviving. By making some small changes to your garden, you can make a big difference to them and to the environment as a whole. *(Help a hedgehog! Save a slug! Befriend a beetle! – Izzie.)* Here are some ideas how:

1 If you're lucky enough to have a decent-sized garden, ask your parents if you can have your own corner to dedicate to growing wildflowers. (You can buy packets of wildflower seeds at any garden centre.) This will provide a habitat for loads of lovely wild creatures.

2 See if you can provide shelter for a particular species: for instance, install a bird box to encourage birds to nest in your garden, or a bat box – bats are an endangered species. They're also natural predators of night-flying insects like moths and flies, so a bat box will help to keep your patio insect-free on summer evenings, leaving you to enjoy your barbecue or simply lounge about with a cool drink watching the sunset unpestered by pesky pests.

3 Add a light-coloured rock to your garden to encourage butterflies to bask on it in the early-morning sun (make sure it's a few feet high for protection against predators), or ask your parents to help you drill holes in a block of untreated wood and hang it under the eaves of your house as a resting spot for tired, solitary bees *(yes, seriously)*.

4 Put out scraps of food for the birds – bits of stale bread, leftover bacon rinds, egg shells etc. will all help birds survive hard winters.

Quick Fix

Providing water in your garden is the number one way to attract wildlife. Persuade your parents to put in a pond if you can, but if that's going a bit too far, don't worry – adding a bird bath is almost as good. You don't have to splash out on a fancy-schmancy stone sculpture – just turn a dustbin lid upside down and fill it with water and all sorts of thirsty little creatures will love you for it.

TOP TIPS FOR GREEN QUEENS

If you're not naturally green-fingered, this one's for you . . . The very best thing you can do in your garden to help save the planet is in fact to do nothing at all! Tell your family that instead of pruning and dead-heading in autumn, it's much better to leave all the dead material in your garden all winter.

❀ This helps to protect the living parts of plants from frost – after all, it's what happens in nature.

❀ It leaves seed heads for birds to nibble on.

❀ The dead stems of plants will provide homes for helpful garden creatures such as ladybirds.

❀ If you have room in your garden, convince your parents to leave one corner as a totally wild, untouched area. All sorts of animals will gratefully use the shelter.

Who would ever have thought that the very best sort of gardening is to do nothing at all?

Tasty Tim's Eco-Facts

On average, every person in Europe throws away the equivalent of two thousand eight hundred banana skins in food waste every year. Read on to find out how to cut down your family's food waste.

Compost Corner

A brilliant way of reducing the amount of rubbish sent to landfill is to scrounge a tiny bit of your garden to turn into a compost heap. It doesn't have to look like a huge stinking mound of rotting food either (which is essentially what a compost heap is – whiff!). You can get neat and tidy compost bins in all sorts of shapes and sizes – many local councils sell them at discount prices or even give them away free. Make it your job to collect your family's food waste and put it in the composter, and spare a couple of hours to sweep up fallen leaves in the autumn and add them too (instead of your dad burning them on a bonfire and contributing to air pollution), and you're well on the way to being a Green Queen. Not only will you be reducing your family's rubbish, but you'll end up with brilliant fertiliser for the garden, which will mean whoever looks after the garden in your house won't have to buy un-green manufactured products. Double yay!

Here's what you can feed your compost heap with:

❀ fruit and vegetable peelings

❀ left-over fruit and vegetables

❀ tea bags

❀ coffee grounds

❀ grass cuttings

❀ hedge trimmings

❀ any other dead plant matter

Don't include meat, cheese or fish, as you'll attract unwanted furry friends such as rats into your garden.

Tasty Tim's Eco-Facts

A dripping tap can waste up to four litres of water every day. An easy problem to solve – turn it off or call the plumber!

Water Good Idea

See if you can collect rain to water your garden, rather than using water from the tap. Ask your parents if you can put a water butt somewhere inconspicuous. You may need some help to install it – it's fairly easy to do (make sure you remember to prop it up on blocks so you can get a watering can underneath!), but it's a bulky thing to handle. So rope in your mates or use it as an excuse to get chatting to a boy or two who can give you a hand. Some local authorities sell cheap water butts, or try www.raincatch.com or www.water-tanks.net.

Tasty Tim's Eco-Facts

In the average household, central heating produces enough carbon dioxide to fill more than 200,000 party balloons. Read on to make sure you're not using more than you need.

Be Warm and Green

One of the best things you can do to save burning fossil fuels and making global warming worse is to make your heating more efficient. This is something you'll need to persuade the rest of the family to get into – they'll thank you for it as it will save them money in the long run.

Here's how:

1 On cold, dark winter nights, go around your house drawing all the curtains and shutting the doors to all the rooms – it's amazing how much toastier this keeps everywhere, and all it takes is a bit of effort.
2 Paste some kitchen foil behind the radiator in your bedroom (and other radiators if your family agree) with the shiny side facing into the room. This acts as a type of insulation by reflecting heat back into the room.
3 Get your parents to turn the thermostat on your central heating down by one degree so that it doesn't come on automatically as often.
4 Make sure that the timer on your hot water heater is only set to times of day when you really need hot water, not on the 'all day' setting.

Quick Fix

Ask your mum or dad if they can set your central heating to cut out thirty minutes before the last person usually goes to bed. It takes a while for a house to cool down, so it should stay comfortably warm until everyone's safely tucked up!

Eco-friendly Laundry

Did you know that every time your clothes are sploshing round in the washing machine, you're using up the planet's water supply and burning fossil fuels for electricity? We didn't. But it doesn't mean that you have to give up washing your clothes and go round smelling niffy in order to save the planet. *(Phew – Nesta.)* All you have to do is be more conscious of the environment when it comes to doing your laundry.

I   Make sure your family only use the washing machine for full loads – if you've got just one or two things that need an urgent wash, do them by hand.

2 Detergents pollute the water system, so encourage your family to use environmentally-friendly washing powders or liquids.

3 Even better, invest in a set of eco washing balls, which you can use instead of washing powder or liquid. *(We're told they work by producing ionized oxygen that gets water molecules to penetrate deep into clothing fibres to lift dirt away – but don't ask us exactly what this means; they just work, OK?)* They may seem expensive, but they last for one thousand washes, so they actually save money in the long term – and, of course, they're much better for the environment. You can buy them from the Internet – just search for 'eco balls'. (Your brother's filthy football kit might be too much of a challenge, though, so keep some eco-washing powder in the cupboard just for extreme cases!)

4 Persuade your family to stop using fabric softeners – they're not necessary, and it just means more chemicals going down the drain – literally.

5 Ask your family to wash their clothes in cooler water, unless they're very dirty. Studies have shown that clothes get just as clean at thirty degrees as at forty degrees, and far less energy is used to heat the water.

6 Whenever possible, hang washing out on the clothes line to dry naturally, instead of using the time-saving but energy-eating tumble drier. (Drying them in the open air makes clothes smell lovely and fresh too.) In colder weather, hang out clothes on an indoor clothes drier or over radiators (if they're on already).

Quick Fix

For an easy way to save water, ask your parents if you can put water-filled plastic bottles in your loo cisterns. It means that the cistern doesn't need so much water to fill it up, so the amount of water used with each flush is reduced.

Tasty Tim's Eco-Facts

Since the 1950s, over seventy-two thousand synthetic chemicals have been introduced into cleaning products. These are poisonous to the environment and don't break down naturally over time. How can we stop this madness? Keep reading . . .

Green Cleaning

Try to cut down on cleaning products because they contain harsh chemicals that are damaging to the environment. *(Yay! I mean, yay, cut down on cleaning because it is way boring, not because it is damaging to the environment – Izzie.)*

Also, using too many cleaning products is actually causing problems such as an increase in childhood asthma and eczema. All this doesn't mean you should cut out cleaning! Instead, suggest to whoever does most of the cleaning in your house *(My mum, she's obsessive – Izzie)* that you can help out on a regular basis, and you want to make a couple of your own cleaning products. No one's ever going to turn down an offer of help with the cleaning. *(You don't know my mum. She likes to do it properly –Izzie.)*

If the thought of cleaning really fills you with horror, just think of all those polar bears you'll be helping . . . *(Why – don't they like cleaning? – Izzie.)*

Here are some home-made cleaning solutions:

❀ To polish furniture, mix together some beeswax, turpentine and your favourite essential oil. *(That would be neroli/orange blossom for me – Izzie.)*

❀ To disinfect surfaces, infuse leaves of rosemary, eucalyptus, lavender, sage and thyme in water. *(They smell really fresh and herby – Izzie.)*

✻ To get rid of kitchen grease, scrub with a mixture of salt and bicarbonate of soda (be careful on delicate surfaces, though, as it could leave scratches).

✻ To make windows and glassware gleam, wash with a solution of one part vinegar to four parts water.

✻ To clean your toilet, pour cheap malt vinegar down the pan – it's excellent for removing limescale and marks.

✻ To shine hardwood floors, brew two teabags in hot water and cool to room temperature, then apply with a mop or cloth (no need to rinse).

✻ *To relax, have a nice cup of herbal tea and a big chunk of organic chocolate . . . Mmm – Izzie.*

Quick Fix

Don't use disposable cloths for dusting or cleaning – this means unnecessary manufacturing and waste. Use washable cloths instead, or, even better, make them yourself from old T-shirts.

Keep it Fresh!

Here are some ideas for keeping your house smelling lovely without using loads of chemicals and unnecessary packaging.

❄ Plants act as natural air filters, so invest in a few houseplants and make it your job to keep them watered and dusted (so they can breathe!).

❄ To get rid of pongy niffs in your home *(Do you know my brothers? – Lucy)*, put a mixture of lemon juice and water into a plastic pump (like the ones you get to spray plants) and get spraying. Or put a few slices of lemon or orange with some cloves and water into a saucepan and simmer for an hour or so.

To freshen up carpets, vacuum, then sprinkle on baking soda, leave it for an hour, then vacuum again.

 Natural aromatherapy candles make anywhere smell gorgeous.

Quick Fix

Take on the job of dusting all the electrical equipment in your home. This will keep the air vents from getting blocked, which would mean they'd use more electricity.

DIY: Cook for the Planet (by TJ)

For a gigantic step nearer Green Queen status, cook eco-friendly meals for your family now and again – but not you, Nesta – we all know about your cooking. *(Cheek – Nesta.)* The secret is to keep it simple. You don't have to fry one thing, grill another and roast two more, all for one meal. You can think much greener than that.

❈ If you use a steamer, you can boil potatoes, steam veggies and heat a sauce all on one gas or electric ring.

❈ You can also use all sorts of manual gadgets instead of electrical ones to save on energy – for instance, don't use a blender to mince food up, just put it through a hand grinder; and don't use an electric can opener – a manual one will do the job just as well.

These may seem like little things, but if you and your mates all make a pact to cook one meal a week for your families, and cook it using green produce and methods, the energy and pollution savings really will mount up.

Our fave easy-peasy green sort of meals are:

1 Salads – it's impossible to burn a salad, so anyone can make one *(Yes, even you, Nesta.)* Make sure your salad is eco-friendly by using locally-grown ingredients, organic if possible.

2 Stir-fries – a stir-fry is cooked very quickly over just one burner, so you're using minimum fuel. Use lots of locally-grown veg, organic if possible.

3 Omelettes – again, an omelette is cooked quickly over just one burner, so you're using minimum fuel. Make sure your eggs are free-range (and preferably organic too), to make sure that your chickens have had an environmentally-friendly, happy life. Bulk up your omelette with tasty locally-grown veg (organic if poss) to make it into a filling meal.

4 Soups and stews – again, you can cook a big pot of health-giving soup or stew over just one burner, using lots of lovely locally-grown produce.

5 Casseroles – another type of 'one-pot' dish, which cooks in the oven, so keeping fuel usage down again.

6 Picnics – there's no better way to eat 'green' food than to get out into nature with your mates and a great excuse to invite some buff boys. Make some sarnies and a tub of salad (which obviously involve little or no cooking at all, so low or no fuel usage), choose some fresh fruit and a big bar of organic chocolate and take some bottled tap water. Make sure you pack everything in reusable containers and don't use plastic plates or cutlery – either take china, washable ones (wrap them up in tea towels so they don't break) or use paper ones you can recycle afterwards. All healthy (so good for a beauty boost) and green at the same time – what more could you ask for!

See pages 49 to 54 for green food shopping tips.

TOP TIPS FOR GREEN QUEENS

Next time you crave a fast food fix, just think about all the packaging which comes along with your mega-burger and fries. What a waste! Resist the temptation, and you'll be doing the planet a favour.

Green Queen Goals

Have a look at our goals and then write your own!

Green things I am going to do TODAY:

Izzie: Ask my mum if we can get a compost bin.

Lucy: Turn down the thermostat on our central heating.

Nesta: Talk to the girls about starting a magazine exchange.

TJ: Find out where to recycle my old mobile phone.

Green things I am going to start doing THIS WEEK:

Izzie: Check out second-hand clothes shops for vintage stuff.

Lucy: Find out what we can recycle locally – what gets collected and where we can take the rest.

Nesta: Organise a clothes-swapping party for all our mates.

TJ: Start making our garden more wildlife-friendly.

Now it's your turn!

Three green things I am going to do TODAY:

1 .... ☆

2 .... ☆

3 .... ☆

Five green things I am going to start doing
THIS WEEK:

1 .... ☆

2 .... ☆

3 .... ☆

4 .... ☆

5 .... ☆

Once you've achieved the above, you'll have
earned the title of Green Queen for sure.
Congratulations, Your Majesty!

CHAPTER 4

Be a Green Goddess

A Note from Nesta

Howdy folks, it's Nesta and I have read and listened and realised that it's not as difficult or boring as I first imagined. Now if, like me, you've got this far with your planet-saving plans, you've done brilliantly. Just keep going and don't look back. If you meet with resistance, don't give up. Remember: when the going gets tough – the tough go shopping. Sorry, old habits die hard. I meant: when the going gets tough – the tough get going and shopping for free-range organic whatnots.

Every time you feel like not bothering to go any
greener than you are, just think of all those giant
pandas and great apes, tigers, elephants and
rhinos, whales and dolphins and marine turtles
you'll be saving (TJ told me that they're all under
threat due to shrinking habitat and pollution).
Think of how you're not contributing to pumping
poisons into the Earth, the seas, the skies. Think
of how you're helping to calm tidal waves, tame
tornadoes and hold back the rising oceans (all
pretty terrifying features of climate change). Feeling
superhuman yet? You should be – just don't go too
extreme and start wearing your underwear over
your jeans like Superman – it was never a cool
look. Where was I? Oh yes, you and your mates
have powers you never knew you possessed. So
here's how to go one stage further and be a Green
Goddess . . .

Compost on, dudes.
Nesta

Go Organic

Being a Green Goddess means *eating* like a Green Goddess. And eating like a Green Goddess means eating organic whenever possible. It can be expensive, but if you grow your own organic fruit and veg, you'll be able to eat it till it comes out of your ears, because it will be much cheaper than in the shops.

Unless you're already into gardening, you might find growing your own too much like hard work. So, instead of trying to hoe it alone, *(arf arf, hoe it alone)* get your mates to join you in rising to the challenge. Even if your own family don't want to dedicate some garden space to a veggie patch, one of your mates' families will probably be keen. Alternatively, you could suggest to a keen green

parent that they rent an allotment and you and your mates could offer to help out. (Allotments are small plots of land rented out to people especially to grow fruit, vegetables and other plants.) Renting one won't break the bank – many councils let them for as little as twenty pounds a year. Sometimes they can be rented privately too.
As a bonus, any boys you meet down the local allotments should be a) thoughtful and caring (well, they obviously care about the environment and about food) and b) very fit (because of all that digging).

In planet-saving terms, you qualify for loads of greenie points (the eco-version of brownie points) if you grow your own because:

❀ you'll be helping the environment by cutting down the amount of pesticides and fertilisers being used on the land (not to mention entering your own body – which can only be a good thing).

❀ you will be providing a home for many different types of wildlife (and I don't just mean eco-friendly boys in the next allotment).

❋ you will be cutting down on pollution from transport, because you aren't buying veg from the shops.

❋ you'll be cutting down on the fuel and carbon emissions involved in making packaging and also cutting down on waste, because you won't need any packaging.

❋ you can grow food which tastes fantastic, unlike many commercial growers who focus on growing food which will last longer.

❋ all that organic fruit and veg will do your appearance a favour – your eyes will be sparkling, your hair will be shining, your skin will be glowing -- and you'll be more toned and gorgeous because of all the exercise.

❋ you can give some of what you grow as gifts and impress people with all your hard work. Most boys will be so impressed when you offer to show them your organic melons.

Tasty Tim's Eco-Facts

Ten per cent of the greenhouse gases emitted into our atmosphere are produced by livestock such as sheep and cattle (yes, from their bottoms – in manure and farting!).

(Ee-ew. Gross – Nesta, Lucy and Izzie. Hope no-one tries to light said sheep's fart as they might blow the planet up. It's the sort of thing my stupid brothers might do – Lucy.) Eating a diet low in meat but high in organic pulses, grains, fruit and veg is better for the environment.

DIY: Grow Your Own

Growing your own veggies can be much easier than you think. *(Agreed– even I've managed to come up with a bumper crop of spuds. Now I just have to resist the urge to turn them all into chips – Izzie.)* It doesn't have to be time-consuming or expensive. A few packets of seeds and some basic tools – a spade, fork, hoe, rake, trowel and watering can and a fit boy to help you with the digging – are all you need to get started and fill a plot with tasty greens. Here are some tips:

1 Borrow some tools if you can, or buy them second-hand from a car boot sale. If you do buy them new, choose tools made from sustainable wood or recycled plastic and rubber, not PVC.

2 You don't need to buy new plastic plant containers to grow seedlings – if you use biodegradable empty cardboard egg boxes, you don't even have to remove them when you plant your seedlings out.

3 Plant wildlife-friendly flowers alongside your veg, to encourage an array of bugs to visit that will help to keep veg-loving pests under control.

4 Fresh herbs such as rosemary and thyme are easy to grow in a small space and will also help encourage bees, butterflies, hover flies and other useful garden insects.

5 You'll want to stop slugs from nibbling your greens, but don't kill them with slug pellets (birds and other wildlife eat slugs, so the toxins in the pellets might be harmful to them too).

Salt pellets will do the job just as well. Even better, put a saucer of beer near to the plants you want to protect. The slugs will get drunk and stay away!

6   To deter hungry snails, sprinkle eggshells and lemon peel around susceptible plants – they are repelled by the smell of lemon and they can't manoeuvre themselves over eggshells. *(Poor little snails – Lucy.)*

7   If you drape fine netting like muslin over your seedlings it will protect them from insects chewing them or laying eggs, and will keep cats and birds away.

8   To keep away ground mammals like rabbits, try sprinkling dried holly leaves around your veg beds – the spikes will hurt their feet and discourage them from approaching, while the leaves will biodegrade over time. *(Now I feel sorry for the bunnies too – Lucy.)*

9   Don't forget to use the rich organic compost you'll have made by now in your composter!

TOP TIPS FOR GREEN GODDESSES

If you and your mates can't go in
for a whole vegetable patch for
any reason, then think small
instead. As Lucy will tell you,
just because things are small
it doesn't mean they can't be
fantastic. You can grow dwarf
varieties of most veggies in
containers just like the ones
used for flowers on patios. You can
grow salad leaves in window boxes. You
can even grow Mediterranean herbs and
peppers indoors, on a sunny windowsill.

Quick Fix

If you can't grow your own organic fruit and veg, there are many companies that deliver organic food in reusable boxes straight to your door. As well as organic food being better for the environment and your health, this cuts down on greenhouse gas emissions from manufacturing, packaging and transport too (just one vehicle is involved in delivering to many families, rather than all those families taking their own car to the supermarket). Start working on your parents . . .

Plant a Tree for the Planet

Hug a tree today – it deserves it! *(OK, now this has gone too far – Nesta.)* A top way to save the planet is to plant a tree. A tree is beautiful to look at. It provides a habitat for all sorts of wildlife. A tree provides shade. And most important of all, a tree creates oxygen while absorbing carbon dioxide from the atmosphere – so the more trees there are on Planet Earth, the more this will help to cancel out the greenhouse effect, global warming and climate change. Just think: if you plant a tree native to your area somewhere local, you can really reduce the amount of carbon dioxide in the air. Some environmental organisations run Tree Parties you and your mates can go along to. At these, you can help plant a tree or two, and also enjoy other events such as picnics and woodland walks. *(How romantic! – Nesta.)* If you and your mates can't find local Tree Parties, have a go at holding them yourselves. Here's how to do it:

1 Offer to plant trees for your families, other friends and neighbours, and invite everyone along to join in and help. The more people you get involved, the more trees you'll be able to plant.
2 If people want trees planted but can't afford to buy them for you to plant, try to raise the money yourself through things like organising a hand car wash on your street or a cake sale at school. Some organisations (such as The Woodland Trust, see www.woodlandtrust. org.uk) even offer grants of a hundred quid or so for tree planting events.

3 Think hard about what kind of tree will suit the chosen spot – hopefully it will be there a looooong time but first of all there are a few things you need to take into consideration:

❀ Ask whoever you're planting the tree for if they know what their soil is like, or buy a soil testing kit from a garden centre. *(Isn't soil just brown and muddy? – Nesta. No, oh non-green-fingered one. It can be acidic, alkali, clay or sandy – get the idea? – TJ.)*

❀ Find out whether the spot is sunny or shady, and whether it's sheltered or exposed to the wind.

❀ Check out the final size of the tree, to make sure it will fit in with the environment – it's not a good idea to have a giant tree close to a house.

❀ Ask a clued-up adult for advice about suitable trees, or check an online gardening site such as www.crocus.co.uk.

4 The best time to plant a tree is autumn, when the tree isn't having a growth spurt but the soil isn't completely wintry cold. Here's what to do when you're ready to plant your tree:

❋ Take the container off the young tree's rootball and dig a hole that's as deep as the rootball and twice as wide. (This is the perfect opportunity to play the weak and feeble girl and ask for help from an oh-so-strong boy or two – after all, all's fair in the art of flirting.)

❋ Loosen the soil around the hole a bit with your shovel.

❋ Place the tree in the hole, making sure the soil is at the same level on the tree as when the tree grew in the garden centre.

❋ Fill in around the rootball with soil and pack the soil with your hands and feet to make sure that there are no air pockets.

❋ Make a little dam around the base of the tree as wide as the hole with leftover soil or grass clumps to hold in the water.

❀ Give your lovely new tree a good soaking of water to help settle it into its new home.

❀ Surround your tree with 'mulch' – a covering of rotten leaves, wood chips, pine straw or shredded bark that will insulate the ground, decrease the amount of weeds that grow, keep moisture around the roots and provide food for your tree.

❀ Be prepared with some flasks of tea/coffee/ soup etc. to hand round to everyone who's helped (either washable cups or paper ones, not plastic, so you can recycle them afterwards). This is another great way to get mingling with any nice-looking boys who have turned up. Tree planted – planet on the way to being saved – new boyfriend in the bag. Result.

Tasty Tim's Eco-Facts

One mature tree can provide enough oxygen for a family of four to breathe for a whole year!

TOP TIPS FOR GREEN GODDESSES

Don't forget that if someone
who would like a tree doesn't
have a garden but does have a
driveway, patio, courtyard or even
a balcony, you can always plant
them a small tree in a container.

- Choose a suitable tree such as
  a Japanese maple, bay, holly or
  magnolia (check online or ask at
  your local garden centre).
- Make sure you have a container with
  good drainage holes.
- Use the right type of potting compost for
  container-grown trees (ask your local garden
  centre again).
- Check that your container is big enough for the
  roots to have room to grow.
- Keep the compost below the top edge of the
  container to stop it flooding out when the tree is
  watered.

Tasty Tim's Eco-Facts

The amount of wood and paper thrown away each year in the United States alone is enough to heat fifty million homes for twenty years. Keep reading to find out how to make sure you're not wasting any.

Create a 'Breathing Place'

If you and your mates *really* like a challenge, see if you can create your own 'breathing place'. This means finding a patch of waste ground in your area, clearing it of rubbish and weeds etc., and transforming it into a healthy green space that improves the health of the environment and gives local people something to enjoy. A breathing place could be anywhere, such as:

❀ a corner of unused land at your school

❀ a bit of derelict ground at the end of your road

❀ any space you walk past every day and think, 'Why doesn't someone clean that up?'

First, you have to find out who owns the land (like it's not someone's neglected garden, for instance). Your local council can tell you if they own the land or if it's owned privately. The Land Registry can help you track down private owners. Once you've found the owners, you have to check that they're happy for you to create a breathing place there, but it's your chance to make something truly wonderful for wildlife – and the local community. It's estimated that there are 70,000 hectares of derelict and vacant land across England and Wales alone – that's an area the size of Greater London just going to waste! Some organisations such as the Big Lottery Fund will give you grants to create a breathing place. So get stuck in and rope lots of other people in to help – any boys who volunteer to get involved are likely to be interesting types with plenty of get up and go. *(Use your common sense and don't hang around waste ground on your own or after dark – TJ.)* This chapter has loads of ideas on what to do once you've found your breathing space.

I love this idea. The Secret Garden *by Frances Hodgson Burnett is one of my all-time favourite books. It's about a lonely girl who transforms a neglected garden into a magical place. If you*

haven't read it or seen the movie, do. I bet it will inspire you to make your own secret garden – Lucy.

Quick Fix

Why not become members of your local nature reserve or conservation group? Environmental organisations are always in need of volunteers to offer their time and effort to help. If you and your mates give up even one afternoon to help pick up litter in a forest, or replant a river bank, or give out campaign leaflets in the shopping precinct, you'll be making a huge difference to local plant and animal welfare (and it's a great way to meet people – as in boys – as you have the perfect excuse for starting up a conversation).

Tasty Tim's Eco-Facts

Thirty-three football-pitch-sized areas of forest are cut down in the world every second. Join an environmental group so you can add your voice to those campaigning for this to stop.

Go Green at School

It's official: going to school is a bad thing. Well, a bad thing for the environment, anyway. Schools in the UK emit five million tonnes of carbon dioxide into the environment every year, just from using gas and electricity. And scientists reckon that schools contribute another five million tonnes of carbon dioxide each year through transport to and from school, and the manufacture of school equipment. *(Hurrah, let's not go then! – Lucy. Er, not what I meant – some schools are doing something about it – Tim. Bummer, I mean, er . . . yeah, cool – Lucy.)* The government has been investing money in turning schools greener, so your school may well already have a green strategy and/or an eco club. If not, now's your chance – you and your mates can start them. And if they have already got one – then join in. You can bring new energy and ideas such as these:

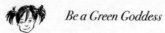

1 Improve your class's recycling.
2 Start up litter patrols to clear up rubbish and make sure that everything that can be recycled is recycled.
3 Carry out a survey on how everyone travels to school, then see how you can make this more eco-friendly. For instance, you could organise a car-sharing rota, or campaign to have more school buses laid on, or raise more money to have new bike sheds built. *(Good excuse to bag a lift with a boy you fancy. See, this green thing opens up a whole new list of chat-up lines – Nesta.)*
4 Find out if there's anywhere in the school grounds that could do with some tree planting.
5 See if you could set up an organic veg patch and set up a rota of volunteers to look after it.
6 Campaign for school governors to switch cleaning products and teaching supplies to environmentally-friendly versions.
7 Start a newsletter to raise awareness of green issues and how you all can contribute to saving the planet outside school.

If you and your mates put your heads together, you can come up with some fantastic schemes to involve the whole community too. *(Lucy, TJ, Izzie*

and I managed to raise thousands of pounds once when we held a charity ball. As one of our fave sayings goes: 'Fortune favours the brave' – Nesta.)

Tasty Tim's Eco-Facts

In the UK, twenty-two per cent of secondary school pupils and forty-one per cent of primary school children are driven to school every day, pumping out carbon dioxide (the most evil greenhouse gas) from their cars. Walk or cycle to school if you can, or take public transport. If those aren't an option, try to set up a car share.

Quick Fix

Persuade your parents to let you remove your family from junk mail lists. You can do this online very easily at www.mpsonline.org.uk. Make sure that when they're filling out forms, if they opt to receive sales and marketing info, they choose to receive it via email rather than the post. And finally, put a big note on your front door saying: 'No junk mail or free newspapers'.

Tasty Tim's Eco-Facts

If each household in the UK changed three of their traditional lightbulbs for energy-saving ones, it would save enough energy to light up all the street lamps in the country.

How To Annoy Your Parents

Yes, this really is part of going green! You know how maddening it is when your parents nag you to do things? It can drive you bonkers – but more often than not you end up doing things their way *(usually because we're right – Izzie's mum)*. Well, here's your chance to get your own back, by putting pressure on non-green parents to do their bit to save the planet. The way to do it is to badger your parents at every available opportunity – in the car, family meals, while watching TV . . . If you want to be really super-annoying you could even stand outside the bathroom door when your mum or dad's on the loo and talk to them through the keyhole – then you've got a captive audience. We can bet parents won't understand things like why, if they buy a hybrid-fuelled car, they'll be helping to ensure that polar bears don't die out, so explain green issues to ensure that your mum and dad get the message too. The best thing about this is that your parents won't actually be able to argue with you – as long as you know your facts, when it comes to green issues, you'll be right and they'll be wrong. *(Excellent – Izzie.)* If that sort of information doesn't get them, try financial reasons – for instance, make sure they know exactly how much money insulating the house better could save them per year . . . Talking money should produce results for sure.

Here's what to try to convince your family about:

1 Get your parents to switch to greener companies for gas and electricity. You can find out how at http://green.energyhelpline.com/energy or www.foe.co.uk/campaigns/climate/press_for_change/choose_green_energy.
2 Help your parents improve the insulation of your home and your family's energy expenditure by researching any grants they might be eligible

for. You can find out at www.energysavingtrust.
org.uk.

3 See if you can get your parents to set up a
system to use your family's grey water (water
which has been used for washing and can be
reused for watering gardens rather than sent
straight down the drain – e.g. water from
laundry, dishwashers, baths, showers, hand-
washing etc.). This can be done easily with a
grey water diverter valve (which enables you to
choose whether you want to send waste water
down the drain or send it to a storage vessel).

4 When it's time to decorate, see if you can
persuade your parents to choose eco-friendly
paints and update fixtures and fittings from
salvage yards, charity shops and websites that
sell second-hand items such as eBay.

5 If it's time to buy new furniture, floorboards or wooden fittings, check that they come from sustainable sources – go to www.fsc.org.

6 Help your parents choose eco-friendly holidays for your family. For instance, camping, nature-watching trips, hiking, boating and cycling holidays, are all good choices. Encourage them to avoid flying if possible. Once you're on holiday, try to help the local community by going to small shops and cafés, rather than spending all your money in big, commercial tourist centres.

Tasty Tim's Eco-Facts

A return flight for two from Amsterdam to the Thai resort of Phuket produces considerably more carbon dioxide than the average new car does in a year. Try not to fly!

Be Car Conscious

✻ If your parents are about to buy a new car, make sure they choose one which gives off less carbon dioxide. They can find advice on www.dft.gov.uk/ActOnCO2

❀ Remind your parents to keep the tyres pumped up well – if they're under-inflated the car has to work harder and will use more fuel.

❀ Make sure there's not loads of clutter in the boot – extra weight uses unnecessary fuel and creates extra carbon dioxide.

❀ Nag your parents if they rev the car up a lot or keep the engine idling when the car isn't moving – these things waste fuel and increase CO_2 emissions.

Green Gadgets

How many gadgets does your family have that they never use? Think about sandwich toasters, plug-in grills, slow cookers, electric carving knives, foot or face spas, electronic toys or electronic gym equipment? Take them to a charity shop (check first that they accept electrical goods) or car boot sale or sell them on eBay. That way, other people can buy them instead of getting new ones.

When your household appliances break, make sure your parents try their best to get them mended, rather than just rushing out to buy new ones. See if you can track down a local repair shop for them – look in the phone directory. And if they do end up buying new, then remind them to go for eco-friendly choices. Energy-efficiency information should be clearly detailed on the labels of appliances in shops.

Tasty Tim's Eco-Facts

You'll be glad to know that the most efficient dishwashers use only one to two units of electricity for a full load, and just fifteen litres of water, whereas washing the equivalent full load by hand would use anything from thirty litres to two hundred litres. So using a dishwasher can be better for the environment than washing up in the sink – as long as your dishwasher is an eco-efficient model and you only run full loads.

TOP TIPS FOR GREEN GODDESSES

Your family's fridge-freezer could
be responsible for about twenty
per cent of your household's total
electricity use; you can tell your
parents how to ensure it is
working efficiently.

Here's how:

- If it is placed near to a radiator
  or the oven, it will use more
  energy, so see if it can be moved
  somewhere cooler.
- Check the manual to see if your fridge is set to the
  correct temperature.
- Make sure that your freezer is defrosted regularly,
  because a build-up of ice may mean the door won't
  shut properly, which will mean the freezer won't be
  working to maximum efficiency.

Tasty Tim's Eco-Facts

*Using an energy-efficient fridge could save half
a tonne of carbon dioxide emissions per year,
compared to an older, less efficient model.*

Quick Fix

Talk your parents out of taking the car through the car wash as it uses a massive amount of water, electricity and chemicals. You might have to offer to wash the car yourself, but think of the brownie points you'll get.

Tasty Tim's Eco-Facts

Did you know that many of the ingredients in washing-up liquid are not biodegradable, so they will exist forever, polluting the environment? Get whoever does the shopping in your house to choose eco-friendly versions, or, better still, lead the way and buy some yourself to show that they work just as well.

Quick Fix

When going for a coffee with your mates, meet in places which use washable mugs and crockery, not disposable ones. That way, you're not adding to the planet's mountains of waste.

 *Be a Green Goddess*

Hold a 'Save the Planet' Party

We love a good party – and what could be better than a 'Save the planet' party? Your guests can come as bits of organic broccoli. Only joking, but this saving the planet business *can* be fun. Try a few of the following ideas and you'll soon be looking more like Kermit's cousin *(Kermit's a frog, they're green, yeah? Izzie)* before you know it.

1 Your party could be a spring picnic, summer garden party, autumn barbecue, or winter supper.
2 Invite everyone you know, young and old. Sing along: 'We are the world, we are its children . . . lalalala.'
3 Make all the invites out of recycled paper, or email or text so that you don't use any paper at all.
4 Use washable crockery and cutlery rather than disposable ones.
5 Make your own party decorations by recycling scrap material into paper chains and streamers.
6 Eat green by making nibbles and drinks from local, unpackaged food. You don't have to be

Jamie Oliver's little sister to impress: homemade dips and veggie sticks, baked potato skins with various toppings, interesting sandwiches and salads, cookies and fairy cakes, and fruit punches and smoothies will all help to get your point across and they'll look and taste great too. *(And you'll score points with the boys here, of course. The way to a man's heart really is through his stomach. I have two brothers so I should know . . . Lucy.)*

7   Hold a 'Why Save the Planet?' pub-style quiz. You can take your questions from all the info we've put together in this book. This will get people thinking while having fun at the same time.

8   Invite everyone to think of something practical that they can do to go green and give a prize for the best one.

9 Put on your most flirty smile and sashay around, asking people to add their names to a sheet on which you've written a pledge. It could say something like:

'I, as a responsible, caring citizen of the world, want to do what I can

to help Planet Earth BEFORE IT IS TOO LATE.

This is my pledge to make a difference!

I shall start with small changes –

for instance, I shall turn the telly and computer off properly

when they're not being used.

And I shall aim for bigger changes –

such as walking or biking instead of using the car, whenever possible.

I hereby promise to try every day to do something to save the planet.

And this is my pledge . . .'

10 As people are leaving, hand them a 'thank you for coming' card (recycled paper, again) with a list of suggestions printed on it for other easy things they can do to go green.

That should get the ball rolling!

11 Collect text or email details of everyone who came, particularly the cute boys. It's a great excuse to get in touch with them again.

Green Goddess Goals

Have a look at our goals and then write your own!

Green things I am going to do TODAY:

Nesta: Check out if there are any Tree Parties near where I live.

TJ: Find out if my school has an eco-club or a green strategy.

Lucy: Put a 'No junk mail' notice on our front door (better check with my mum first).

Izzie: Offer to defrost the freezer.

Green things I am going to start doing THIS WEEK:

Lucy: Researching greener gas and electricity for our house.

Izzie: Persuade my mum to get organic fruit and veg delivered.

Nesta: Find out about recycling at school.

TJ: Join the local conservation group.

Now it's your turn!

Three green things I am going to do TODAY:

1 .... ☆

2 .... ☆

3 .... ☆

Five green things I am going to start doing
THIS WEEK:

1 .... ☆

2 .... ☆

3 .... ☆

4 .... ☆

5 .... ☆

When you've managed all these, you'll have truly
earned the title of Goddess of Green. TJ, Lucy, Izzie
and I salute you. All hail!

Afterword

A Note from Us

When we hear about what Planet Earth *might* be like in the future, it can feel very scary.

Extreme weather such as tornadoes, rainstorms and heatwaves . . . rubbish heaps and landfill sites taking up more and more space . . . thousands of species of wildlife becoming extinct as their habitats disappear . . . droughts in some parts of the world and floods in others . . . people struggling for survival . . .

Horrible. But it doesn't have to be like that.

The good news – no, the *great* news – is that scientists say that it's not too late. It's in our power to stop all this from occurring. If we act NOW. We think it's possible. *(Even me now – Nesta.)* We do believe that we can save the planet – if we each do what we can – and straight away.

Unfortunately, our parents' generation isn't doing enough to give everyone a good future on our planet. So we have to shoulder some of the responsibility and take matters in hand – and we've got to start NOW. Do what we can in our own lives, and keep talking to our mates, families, teachers and anyone else we know, so that they make changes in *their* lives. And if *everyone* keeps talking about the future of the planet and demanding bigger changes, the politicians will have to act. It's up to all of us.

Here's one of Lucy's mum's fave bits of wisdom, which is now one of ours too:

There were four people named Everybody, Somebody, Anybody and Nobody.

There was an important job to be done and Everybody was asked to do it.

Everybody was sure Somebody would do it.

Anybody could have done it but Nobody did it.

Somebody got angry about that, because it was Everybody's job.

Everybody thought Anybody could do it but Nobody realised that Everybody wouldn't do it.

It ended up that Everybody blamed Somebody when Nobody did what Anybody could have done.

We'll leave the last word up to Izzie, because the songs she writes always say things best. Thanks for reading, for sharing our ideas and for joining up with us on our mission.

Wishing you all health, harmony and good fortune.

Lots of luv

Bye for now

Lucy, Izzie, Nesta and TJ

XXXX

Save the Planet

by Izzie Foster

Imagine a world with clean green seas,
with clean green fields and clean green trees,
with clean green energy and clean green waste,
with clean green food with a clean green taste,
with clean green peace under clean green skies
'cause we're clean green girls and clean green guys.

Imagine this world for me and for you,
for all of our kids, grandkids – great-grandkids too!
Imagine this world – all clean green and new.
Now let's get together and make it come true.

Eco-friendly Websites

www.aboutorganics.co.uk
A guide to everything organic – including skin care, clothing, gardening and food.

www.bigbarn.co.uk
This website tells you where you can get food from local producers, such as farmers' markets.

www.bafts.org.uk
This is the website of the British Association for Fair Trade Shops. It gives you lots of information about fair trade products and where you can buy them.

www.bbc.co.uk/breathingplaces
Help turn waste ground into a healthy green space.

www.bbc.co.uk/food/in_season
Tells you which foods are in season each month.

www.the-body-shop.co.uk
The website of the Body Shop, environmentally-minded retailer of beauty products.

www.carbonfootprint.com
This website helps you calculate, reduce and offset your carbon footprint.

www.cleanslateclothing.co.uk
Get your fair trade and organic school uniform here.

www.bbc.co.uk/climate
Find out more about climate change.

www.communitycompost.org
Great advice about how to make compost at home.

www.dft.gov.uk/ActOnCO2
Information on which cars have the lowest carbon emissions, and advice on how to minimise your car's damage to the environment.

www.eatlessmeat.org
Info on why we should all eat less meat and advice on how to do it, including lots of lovely vegetarian recipes.

www.theecologist.org
A great website which covers all the issues.

www.energysavingtrust.org.uk
Information on how you can save energy at home.

www.fairtrade.org.uk
Explains how fair trade works, and how to find fair trade products.

www.fishonline.org/advice/eat
Lists which fish are OK to eat, and which are endangered and should be avoided.

www.foe.co.uk
The website of Friends of the Earth, an organisation which campaigns for solutions to environmental problems.

www.freecycle.co.uk
This is an online community you can join for free to advertise items you no longer need to other people in your local area, and find things you need that other local people may have and no longer want!

www.fsc.org
The Forest Stewardship Council, which has advice on buying furniture and other wooden products from sustainable sources.

www.greenchoices.org
Info on how to be greener in loads of areas of your life, including energy, recycling, clothes and pets.

www.greenguideonline.com
Thousands of listings for sustainable and green goods, services and organisations.

www.greenpeace.org
Greenpeace is an organisation that campaigns on the whole range of environmental issues.

www.mpsonline.org.uk
Register with the Mail Preference Service to avoid receiving junk mail and thereby reduce paper waste.

www.oxfam.org.uk/shop
The online shop of charity Oxfam has a huge variety of green and fair trade gifts.

www.polarbearsinternational.org
This website will give you information on polar bears and how to get involved with helping them.

www.recycle-more.co.uk
Find your nearest recycling centre and get info on what materials you can recycle there.

www.recyclingappeal.com
The Recycling Appeal collects mobile phones and printer cartridges for reuse and recycling.

http://www.responsibletravel.com
Promotes ethical tourism.

www.savetheorangutan.org.uk
The website of the Borneo Orangutan Survival Foundation UK,
which works to save orangutans from extinction and prevent the
forests they live in from being destroyed.

www.sustrans.org.uk
The site of the UK's leading sustainable transport charity, which
will tell you about the benefits of cycling and show you where
your nearest cycle routes are.

www.think-energy.co.uk
A website which encourages young people to be more energy
efficient.

www.wasteonline.org.uk
Info and facts about waste disposal in the UK, including details for
companies that recycle computers and electrical equipment.

www.waterwise.org.uk
Info on how to reduce water usage at home.

www.whyorganic.org
Tips on growing your own organic fruit and veg and details of
organic companies.

www.woodland-trust.org.uk
The Woodland Trust is a charity dedicated to preserving Britain's
trees and forests. This website gives details of how you can get
involved, including info on tree planting events and how you can
organise your own.

www.yptenc.org.uk
The website of the Young People's Trust for the Environment,
which gives info about all sorts of environmental issues and how
you can help.

Glossary

Acid Rain
When chemical compounds containing nitrogen and sulphur are released into the atmosphere (such as during some manufacturing processes) they dissolve in the water in the atmosphere to form nitric and sulphuric acid. This falls as acid rain, which eats into trees and buildings and damages them. It also changes the nature of the soil, making it harder for plants to grow.

Biodegradable
Something that is biodegradable breaks down physically and/or chemically over time.

Biological pest control
In agriculture or gardening, this is controlling pests by introducing other creatures which prey on them, instead of using chemical pesticides.

Carbon dioxide
CO_2 is a colourless, odourless gas that occurs naturally in the Earth's atmosphere. It is the main greenhouse gas, which contributes to global warming.

Carbon footprint
Carbon footprints measure how much carbon dioxide we produce just by going about our daily lives (doing things like driving in a car and heating our homes).

Carbon neutral
If you are carbon neutral, you balance the emissions of carbon dioxide you cause just by going about your daily life (travelling by car, having the central heating on etc.) by removing the same amount of carbon from the atmosphere. For instance, you could plant trees, which absorb carbon dioxide as they grow and give out oxygen.

Glossary

Climate change
Global warming is causing the Earth's climate to change, having widespread impacts all over the world, causing more droughts, tornadoes, storms, floods and other weather extremes. This has disastrous implications for all living things on the planet.

Deforestation
Destruction of wooded areas by the cutting down or burning of trees.

Fair trade
This is a movement that ensures that people in the developing world are getting a fair deal for their products and that these are being produced in an environmentally-friendly way.

Food chain
This is a description of how animals and plants are linked by their food relationships, e.g. humans eat chickens, which eat insects and seeds. If seeds are treated with pesticides and fertilisers, humans may effectively be eating those too when they eat chickens.

Food miles
This means the number of miles food travels from where it is made to where it is eaten. Food that is transported a long way involves huge fuel emissions, which increase greenhouse gases, which increase global warming, which increases climate change. Food that travels a long distance also needs more protective packaging to keep it in a decent state, so it's a double whammy for the environment.

Fossil fuels
The three fossil fuels are coal, oil and natural gas. We burn these to produce energy. When they are burned, these components mix with oxygen in the atmosphere. The result is carbon dioxide.

Genetically modified
Genetically modified plants have been scientifically altered to increase their yield or quality. Many people are worried about the long-term effects this will have on animals and humans, as these are not yet known.

Global warming
The Earth's climate naturally changes over long time periods, swinging from long Ice Ages to shorter, warmer periods. However, recently, scientific data suggests that the Earth is warming quickly because of human activity, rather than naturally and slowly. This is global warming. This means that species have not had time to adapt and nature can no longer cope. Global warming leads to long-term climate change.

Greenhouse gases
Greenhouse gases are chemicals that occur naturally and form a blanket around the Earth, trapping heat that would otherwise escape into space. The heat rebounds onto the Earth's surface, and the planet's temperature rises – creating what is commonly called the greenhouse effect. Industrial processes have released more greenhouse gases into the atmosphere, which has increased the Earth's temperature – this is global warming, which causes climate change.

Grey water
Water which has been used for washing (e.g. water from laundry, baths, showers etc.) and can be reused e.g. to water gardens rather than sent straight down the drain.

Hybrid car
Hybrid cars use a combination of electric and petrol/gas power. They are better for the environment than cars which run entirely on petrol; however the electricity they use has to come from the owner's usual electricity source, which will usually be a power plant that burns fossil fuels.

Glossary

Landfill
A landfill site is a large, outdoor burial pit for rubbish.

Methane
Methane is the main component of natural gas. It is also formed by the digestive processes of livestock (i.e. it is emitted by cows and sheep farting!). It has twenty-three times the global warming potential of carbon dioxide.

Organic food
Food that is grown or raised without the use of chemical fertilisers, pesticides, or drugs.

Ozone
A form of oxygen found high up in the Earth's atmosphere, which is responsible for filtering out much of the sun's harmful ultraviolet radiation. Chemicals produced by human activity have thinned the ozone layer over the Earth, exposing parts to this harmful radiation.

Pesticide
Any chemical that is used to protect crops by killing the living creatures which eat them. (Herbicides are chemicals that destroy weeds. Fungicides are chemicals which destroy fungal infections on crops.)

Pollution
Any release into the environment of toxic substances harmful to human health and ecosystems. Transport is responsible for much of the Western world's pollution and greenhouse gas emissions.

Recycle
Recycling turns materials that would otherwise become waste into useful new products. Making new items from recycled ones takes less energy and other resources than making products from brand new materials. Find out what recycling facilities there are where you live by looking up your local council's website.

Reduce

This means creating less waste – by buying and using fewer things, and making sure that anything you do buy is well made (so it will last longer) and not over-packaged. This is the best way (even better than reuse and recycling) to cut down on rubbish, because if you reduce the amount you use in the first place, you'll have less to throw away. Reduce also means saving resources such as electricity and water.

Reuse

Reuse involves giving items a longer life by repairing them, finding new uses for them (e.g. using glass jars and other containers for storage), donating them to charity, or giving or selling them to anyone who needs them. Reuse is even better than recycling, because the item does not need to be reprocessed before it can be used again.

Index

Cathy Hopkins

Like this book?
Become a mate today!

Also available by Cathy Hopkins

The MATES, DATES series

1. Mates, Dates and Inflatable Bras
2. Mates, Dates and Cosmic Kisses
3. Mates, Dates and Portobello Princesses
4. Mates, Dates and Sleepover Secrets
5. Mates, Dates and Sole Survivors
6. Mates, Dates and Mad Mistakes
7. Mates, Dates and Pulling Power
8. Mates, Dates and Tempting Trouble
9. Mates, Dates and Great Escapes
10. Mates, Dates and Chocolate Cheats
11. Mates, Dates and Diamond Destiny
12. Mates, Dates and Sizzling Summers

Companion Book:
Mates, Dates Guide to Life
Mates, Dates and You
Mates, Dates Journal
Mates, Dates and Flirting (coming soon)

The TRUTH, DARE, KISS OR PROMISE series

1. White Lies and Barefaced Truths
2. Pop Princess
3. Teen Queens and Has-Beens
4. Starstruck
5. Double Dare
6. Midsummer Meltdown
7. Love Lottery
8. All Mates Together

The CINNAMON GIRL series

1. This Way to Paradise
2. Starting Over
3. Looking for a Hero

Find out more at www.piccadillypress.co.uk
Join Cathy's Club at www.cathyhopkins.com

Cinnamon Girl 🌿

This Way to Paradise

Cathy Hopkins

Meet India Jane.
Known to her friends and big, chaotic family as
Cinnamon Girl. Born in India, she's lived all over
the world. But what she really wants is to stop
travelling and have a real home.

Just when it looks as though she'll get her wish,
her father lands a job which means the family are on
the move again. So India Jane is sent off to her aunt's
new age holiday centre for the summer. It could be
paradise – but India Jane feels alone and confused.

Should she party with her rebellious cousin, Kate?
Or search for inner peace with the meditation crowd?
And will mystery boy Joe help India Jane discover
where her true happiness lies?

Praise for Cathy Hopkins:

'*Perfect escapist young teenage reading.*' TIME OUT

'*Cathy Hopkins explores, with wit and humour,
important issues for teenagers.*' BOOKS